Sharon's heart began to pound, and she could feel the adrenaline pumping. Her breaths were short, forming trails of mist around her face. She wore only her nightgown, as always, and the air was cold and damp. Despite this, a thin trickle of sweat crawled down her back. She rubbed at it, feeling her hand go clammy at the touch. Her gaze flitted here and there, but nothing moved—yet.

This was the way that it always began. And it always ended the same way, with her—

A sound!

Sharon twisted around, vainly trying to make out something, anything, in those disjointed trees. She tried to call out, but her throat wouldn't obey. She could feel her heart speeding up, pounding. Her breath hissed in and out of her nostrils, the only sound she could hear. Wildly, her eyes darted across the eerie landscape. Nothing.

Also by Nicholas Adams
Available from HarperPaperbacks

Santa Claws
Horrorscope

Don't miss the **HORROR HIGH** series

#1 *Mr. Popularity*
#2 *Resolved: You're Dead*
#3 *Heartbreaker*
#4 *New Kid on the Block*
#5 *Hard Rock*
#6 *Sudden Death*
#7 *Pep Rally*
#8 *Final Curtain*

Also available from HarperPaperbacks

THE VAMPIRE DIARIES
L.J. Smith

Volume I *The Awakening*
Volume II *The Struggle*
Volume III *The Fury*
Volume IV *Dark Reunion*

I.O.U.

Nicholas Adams

HarperPaperbacks

A Division of HarperCollinsPublishers

HarperPaperbacks *A Division of* HarperCollins*Publishers*
10 East 53rd Street, New York, N.Y. 10022

Produced by Daniel Weiss Associates, Inc.
33 West 17th Street, New York, New York 10011.

First printing: August 1991

Manufactured in the United Kingdom by
HarperCollins*Publishers* Inc.

HarperPaperbacks and colophon are trademarks of
HarperCollins*Publishers*

10 9 8 7 6 5 4 3

ONE

Midnight. There was no moon, and the stars were gone. Silence clung to her. For a heartbeat, Sharon did not know where she was. Then, as a chill wind ruffled her hair, she recognized the woods.

The nightmare was back again.

She looked around, feeling the panic begin as a dull throb in her chest. She saw the same dead trees, branches clawing for the skies: leafless, lifeless, but somehow malicious. Like skeletons with evil eyes, all watching her. The ground underfoot was hard and dry. Any grasses or flowers had died and withered long ago. All that were left were roots and stones, all cold, hard, and waiting for her to begin to run.

Sharon's heart began to pound, and she could feel the adrenaline pumping. Her breaths were short, forming trails of mist around her face. She wore only her nightgown, as always, and the air was cold and damp. Despite this, a thin trickle of sweat crawled down her back. She rubbed at it, feeling her hand go clammy at the touch. Her gaze flitted here and there, but nothing moved—yet.

This was the way that it always began. And it always ended the same way, with her—

A sound!

Sharon twisted around, vainly trying to make out something, anything, in those disjointed trees. She tried to call out, but her throat wouldn't obey. She could feel her heart speeding up, pounding. Her breath hissed in and out of her nostrils, the only sound she could hear. Wildly, her eyes darted across the eerie landscape. Nothing.

Wavering, Sharon took a step backward. Her ankle caught on a root, and she almost lost her balance. She looked down, but there was nothing to see. She glanced up again at the trees.

They were there.

Sharon knew it, even though she couldn't see them. They had arrived, and were there, in the woods, somewhere. The man, the dark man, with his brooding eyes and slow, steady tread. And . . . the other. The un-man, the shapeless *thing* that plucked at the edge of her mind but refused to be seen.

Backing up another step, Sharon felt something grab at her long, blond hair. This time she found her voice and screamed, pulling forward. The twigs from the tree jerked free as she spun to face her attacker. Just a tree.

This time.

Again, she felt that they were watching her, waiting for her nerves to break. Waiting for her to run. But this time, she vowed, she wouldn't do it. This time she would be strong. She wrapped her arms around her, as if pulling a cloak over her flimsy clothing. The chill from the ground was numbing her toes. Wriggling them, she tried to fight off the cold. Slowly, hesitantly, feeling ahead with her left hand, she started to walk. She *would not* run! Not this time.

Her fingers touched something cold, clammy, and *alive*. With a start, she drew back. Nothing happened, but she could feel something icky on her fingers. Ugh! Her fingers felt filthy, contaminated, but there was nowhere to wipe them except her filmy nightgown.

She could feel their eyes, watching, waiting, looking for her reaction. Trying to stay rational, Sharon bent down in the darkness, feeling with her itching left hand for something, anything. Her fingers closed on something hard and rounded. As she started to rub the stuff onto whatever it was, the object suddenly came to life, skittering away from her. With a scream, Sharon shot upright, her chest heaving. Without conscious thought, she pulled her left hand close, smearing her fingers onto the gown.

Terrific. She could sense the contaminated spot where it touched her thigh. It made her skin crawl, just knowing it was there. And she could smell it now, a rancid odor of decay, sickly, and growing stronger.

She took a step forward, but of course the smell moved with her. It was the stench of death, of something rotting, and she had touched it. . . .

The icy breeze stirred at her again, brushing her

skin. A shock passed up her body, and she shivered. It was impossible to get warm.

Unless she ran. And she wouldn't do that.

Something crawled across her foot. Something chittering, with dozens of tiny, fast-moving feet. She gasped and tried to kick it away. Something else, wavering, hesitant, reached out to touch her other foot. Sharon spun around, choking back tears, and bony fingers grabbed at her hair. She'd backed into the trees again. With a sob, she pulled herself free.

The scampering things in the darkness started to move again. Insects, bugs, all after her because she was warm and the only living thing in these woods.

Forgetting her resolve, Sharon turned and ran, trying to protect her face from the stinging blows of branches and twigs. Her feet pounded across the uneven ground, stumbling over the rocks and roots that tried to grab at her and pull her down to the dead soil. Her breathing was short, hard, burning pants now, as she strove to fight down the terror welling up within.

Blindly, she dashed onward. She fought off the clutching branches, heedless of the scrapes she was getting. Her legs felt dozens of tiny scratches from the brambles and thorns. She knew she was filthy, bloody, and soaked with perspiration. The twigs tore at the nightgown, dragging at it as she ran. But she couldn't stop. Not now.

Her chest and lungs burned with every short, coughing breath she took. She could feel the punishment the soles of her feet were taking as she ran across the jagged stones and twisting roots. Arms flailing, Sharon ran, the terror growing within her. She wanted to scream, but she had no breath to spare.

It was a hunt, she knew: Her pursuers were in no rush. They wanted her exhausted, ready to break, before they closed in. But knowing it and being able to fight it weren't the same thing. After all, she knew that this was only a dream, but the terror and the lacerations felt very real indeed.

Finally, Sharon could go on no more. For one last time, she stumbled, and now she fell. She couldn't even feel renewed pain as she crashed to the ground. She managed to force one arm under her shaking body and slowly levered herself into a sitting position beneath a skeletal tree. The branches over her head felt like the bars of a cage, and she knew that she was trapped.

Every breath she took burned all the way down to her stomach, and she would never be able to take in enough air. She brushed her long hair away from her eyes and stared out into the darkness.

He was there, watching. Though there was no real light, she could see his eyes burning red as he stared at her. It was the same man as always—tall, dark, with long, shaggy hair flapping in the breeze. His skin was pale, his red eyes sunken. She took all of this in without thinking, because her eyes were drawn to the blade he held.

It wasn't a normal knife. It was more like a cake knife, with a narrow blade that flattened out, then came to a sharp point. Dimly, Sharon knew she had seen something like this knife before, and that it was important. But she couldn't place it. Besides which, this wasn't the time for cold, analytical thought.

This was when she always died.

A slow smile crossed the man's face, twisting it unevenly. He had caught her thought, could scent her panic and utter weariness. He took a step forward, and Sharon tried pathetically to crawl away. But the tree behind her held her firm. The blade rose, ready.

If it was only death that she had to face, she would almost welcome it at this point. The panic had built to fever pitch, and she knew that dying of fright wasn't simply an expression. The thumping of her heart against her rib cage told her that it was almost ready to burst. But death wouldn't be the end . . .

Behind her killer, still hardly there, was the Unseen. It lurked, just on the edges of vision, shifting, hungering, waiting. It was the force behind the man, the predator waiting for its next victim to be delivered. It was ravenous, waiting to devour her, body and soul.

Death would be only the beginning of her agonies.

The knife rose as the man stepped forward. Sharon flung her hand out, a futile gesture she was unable to halt. He laughed and grabbed at her wrist. She cried aloud with the pain as he forced her arm aside. Then, in a frenzy of movement, he struck, plunging the glittering blade straight for her.

At the last second, she screamed.

* * *

6

And shot bolt-upright in her bed, panting, sweating, clutching the sheets around her for protection. Her eyes flew open into the darkness of her bedroom. She could see the shapes and shadows of her precious, familiar life in the gray light coming through the window. The canopy of her bed overhead felt protective, unlike the tree she had just died under. The warmth of the bedclothes she gripped tightly to herself was so comforting. The—

Twin red spots burned in the shadows by the door.

He was here, in her room! He had escaped from her dream! He—

She fought down the terror that reared up within her and moved slightly to get a better look. Then she sighed with relief.

It was the light from her digital clock hitting the mirror on the far wall. There wasn't anyone in the room with her, after all. She was alone, and her parents were across the hall from her, and she was safe. Utterly, utterly safe. It had just been a dream.

Then the redness winked out.

Terror started to build again. Sharon could feel something in the room, something malevolent, something watching her, savoring the smell of her fear. She couldn't turn her head to see. If she didn't look, maybe, maybe she'd be wrong, and it wouldn't be there.

If the redness had been the alarm clock in the mirror, why had it suddenly vanished?

Refusing to surrender to the childish urge to dive under the bedcovers and cry, she fought the tense muscles in her neck, slowly managing to twist her head around to look at the clock.

The front wasn't lit at all. Then, as she stared, the red numbers came back to life, blinking 12:00, over and over.

She let her breath out in one long rush. It had been a momentary power failure, nothing more. The figures flashed on and off now, demanding to be taken care of, and Sharon reached out a hesitant hand for her watch. She half expected something to dart out of the gloom and grab her, but nothing did. She glanced at the watch face but could make nothing out. It was too dark. She switched on the bedside lamp and quickly glanced around her room. Everything was normal, just as it had been when she had turned off the light to go to sleep.

Three thirty-two in the morning! She brushed her hair back and reached over, setting the alarm again. Then she took a drink of the water on her night table. One last look around, to be certain that all was fine, then she reached for the light.

And hesitated. Maybe she'd be better off leaving it on for the last couple of hours of the night? Then she took a grip on her fears and refused to revert to her childhood dread of the darkness. There was nothing there to harm her, nothing at all. It had just been a bad dream that she'd been having.

For the fourth time.

Sharon hastily switched off the light and buried herself under the bedcovers again. But her night-gown stuck to her where she had been sweating, and she wriggled uncomfortably. She was exhausted, as if she'd really been running those terror-filled miles in the eerie forest. And her feet hurt. She rubbed at her left sole, trying to ease the cramping sensations. It didn't help much. It felt rough and sore, almost as if she had been racing through woods in her bare feet. With a sigh of relief, she was just glad that there wasn't any blood or scratches on her body. If there had been, she just might have given in to the panic that lurked slightly beyond the threshold of her consciousness. Sharon was afraid to return to sleep, in case the dream came back. Maybe she'd just stay awake until the morning. . . . Slowly, without being aware of it, she drifted into a dreamless slumber for the remainder of the night.

TWO

"Girl, you look *terrible*," Chiku Williams said.

Sharon glared at her friend. "Thanks a lot. I really needed to hear that this morning."

Chiku laughed. "Hey, what's a best friend for?" Then she sobered, and touched Sharon gently on the arm. "Have you been having that dream again?"

Clutching her school books as if for protection, Sharon nodded. She bit at her lip, almost drawing blood. "Twice more this week, Chiku."

The other girl stared into Sharon's blue eyes and shook her dark head. "You're losing a lot of sleep over it. Maybe you should see a doctor, get something to help you—"

"My parents already suggested that." Sharon sighed. "It's not that bad," she lied. "I can handle it. It's just—oh, one of those things, I guess."

"Recurring dreams?" Chiku snorted. She rubbed at her hair, dislodging one of the garish clips she always wore. This one was a purple butterfly. She adjusted it and continued speaking. "Look, you know my dad's a professor in anthropology and folklore. Some of his brains have rubbed off on me, despite everything I've done to avoid it. You can't tell me that it's perfectly normal for you to have this recurring dream about some slasher stalking you through woods at night and expect me to just believe it. Dreams aren't like that." She smiled, almost apologetically. "Dad's pretty interested in dreams, and he tries his latest ideas out on me first. He says if I can understand them, then any second-year college kid should stand a chance. I think there's more to this gross-out dream than—"

"Just drop it, okay?" Sharon answered sharply. Then, seeing the hurt look on her friend's face, she added: "Honest, Chiku, I can handle it."

"You're not doing too well so far," the black girl said bluntly. "You think I haven't noticed that your grades are slipping?" She tried a grin. "I know I always wanted to beat your GPA, but I'd rather do it by myself, without your help."

"It's time for class." Sharon started to move into the building, but Chiku wouldn't let it rest.

"Sharon, don't be foolish. Get some help."

"Who could I get to censor my dreams?" Sharon shook her head. "Look, I know you're trying to be a friend, but trust me—I can handle this."

Chiku wasn't convinced, obviously, but before she could say anything else, she was distracted by a boy calling her name. Glancing around, she saw Larry Wauchop approaching and groaned very theatrically. "I knew I should have called in sick today."

"Hiya, Cheeky." He grinned, shuffling his books back and forth. "Hi, Sharon."

"Morning, Larry," Sharon said with a smile, glad of the interruption. Larry was in their class and had been nursing a serious crush on Chiku for several months. It had survived the recent summer break and was apparently stronger than ever, judging from the cow eyes he was making at her. Larry was a nice enough guy, though Sharon thought he wasn't quite Chiku's type. He was fairly athletic, but lacked any sign of a tan due to his habit of spending most of his free time watching videotapes. If he had any other interests in life, he'd never mentioned them. Aside from his crush on Chiku, that was.

"How about coming over tonight?" he asked Chiku eagerly. "Got a new flick yesterday—*Zombie Amazon High*. It's supposed to be real scary."

"Right." Chiku laughed. "I'll tell you—if I were in a dark room with you, then I'd be scared. Ask me again some other time. Maybe in about fifty years."

"Right," Larry agreed. "Play hard to get. I love a girl who's not easy." He gave a salute and started to move off to his first class.

"I'm not only not easy," Chiku yelled at his back. "I'm completely unattainable!"

"You know you're crazy about me really," he called back.

Chiku glanced at Sharon, who was trying to hide her smile. "Ain't he cute?" she asked.

Sharon laughed. "Then why not go out with him?"

"What?" Chiku pulled a mock shocked face.

"And have him think I'm a pushover? Not a chance. Anyway, I'm not into those semi-porn slasher flicks he watches. I'm holding out until he asks me to the Halloween Dance."

"What if all this playing hard to get puts him off and he takes someone else?"

Chiku deadpanned back: "No chance! He's nuts about me. Can't you tell? He'll ask me, you wait and see."

"Thus speaks the expert."

"Right." Chiku dug her elbow in Sharon's ribs. "Maybe that's what you need to take your mind off those dreams, girl. I'll have to see about setting you up with a hot-and-heavy date."

"I can find my own boyfriends, thank you," Sharon said, with a little more snap in her voice than she had intended. But it was impossible to insult Chiku.

"Well, so where are they?" she asked. "You've turned down five guys this year already—and that's just the ones that I know of. You training to be a nun or something?"

"It's not that." Sharon couldn't tell her the real reason—that she was afraid of seeing *anyone* while the dream kept coming back. It had started almost as soon as the school year had, and she found it hard to even look at a boy without imagining him holding a knife, coming after her at night. It was a foolish fear, but very, very real.

"Well, take some advice from me," Chiku replied. "Play a little hard to get. Tease 'em and flirt a bit. Show 'em that they have to put some effort into it.

You'll be amazed at how well it works. Guys love a challenge." She winked. "Free advice from the doctor of love, child."

Sharon was about to reply when she got an eerie feeling that she was being watched. The hair on her neck was itching, as if something was stirring at it, and the muscles in her shoulders were tensing up. Slowly, she turned around and saw that the feeling wasn't false.

He was tall, already a few inches over six feet. From his build, he worked out in the gym a lot. His dark hair was neatly trimmed back, and his brown eyes almost blazed. He was handsome, confident, and watching her carefully. Sharon felt a thrill of some strange emotion pass through her. It was like ice, but pleasant, almost addictive. He saw her eyes lock on his, and gave a slow, lazy smile before starting toward them.

Chiku had spotted the move and nudged Sharon. "Way to go, kid. You've got this one panting already. Remember what I told you—play hard to get. He'll lap it up."

The stranger stopped a few feet away from them, his eyes still fastened on Sharon. Finally he spoke.

"Hi. I'm Travis Hale."

Awkwardly, Sharon switched her books to her left arm and held out her right hand. "Sharon Anders."

"I know," he told her. His voice had a trace of an accent, but she couldn't place it. He wasn't a local, that was for sure. "I spotted you a few days back and asked around," he explained. "I wanted to meet you. You're the prettiest girl I've seen since I arrived in town." He looked her over again, and Sharon blushed. His eyes seemed to be drinking her in. "And since I was born," he added.

Sharon felt foolish for being embarrassed, but his eyes had a weird effect on her. It was like he was seeing into her mind and liking what he saw there. Normally she could think of witty replies, or smart conversation, but she was at a total loss here. "Thank you," was all she could manage. Even that was more like a whisper than a reply.

Chiku coughed rather loudly and punched Sharon's arm. Bewildered, Sharon suddenly remembered her friend. "Oh, this is my best friend, Chiku Williams," she said quickly.

"Chiku?" he repeated, turning his eyes away from her to study the black girl. Sharon felt that she could breathe again—and missed being able to look into those brown pools. "An unusual name," Travis added.

"I'm an unusual girl." Chiku grinned. "My name's Kenyan—my family roots. It means *cheerful* or *chatterer*." She winked. "Perfect for me." She was quite clearly turning on the charm, and Sharon felt a sudden pang of jealousy.

He's mine! she thought savagely, wishing Chiku could hear her. Then she was shocked at her thought. Looking up, she saw that, politely, Travis was ignoring the mild flirting Chiku was indulging in, and she relaxed.

"I'd be inclined to agree," Travis replied to Chiku's last remark, then turned back to stare at

Sharon again. "Listen, how'd you like to go out on Saturday? I've got a couple of tickets to—"

"I'd love to," she said in a rush. It didn't matter what they were for—she had an overwhelming desire to spend some time with him. Any time with him. She felt almost giddy, drunk with strange emotions.

Travis smiled. "Okay. I'll call you on Friday." He started to turn away, then added: "But I guess I'll see you around?"

"I hope so," Sharon replied. She felt depressed as he turned to walk away. It was as if thunderclouds had blocked out the sun. She sighed.

"Oh, real cool," Chiku snorted. "You really took my advice there, didn't you? If that's your idea of playing hard to get, I'd hate to think what you'd do if I'd suggested being forward. You'd probably have attacked him in the corridor."

"What?" Sharon was suddenly aware that Chiku had been speaking. "Isn't he *gorgeous*?"

"Him?" Chiku shrugged. "Not my type," she lied, as casually as she could manage.

"Well, he sure is mine."

Chiku raised her eyes to the heavens in mute appeal. "I wonder how I could have guessed that? What has come over you? One minute, you're telling me that you're not interested in dating, and the next you're about to faint over the slightest attention from this guy."

"Don't be silly," Sharon said. "It's not like that at all. It's just . . ." Her voice dried up as she thought about it. Why had she agreed so readily? All she could think of were those dark, romantic eyes.

"Just what?" Chiku prompted. "Lack of sleep affecting your emotions?"

"I know what I'm doing," Sharon said firmly. *I hope*, she added mentally. She'd never acted like this before. But she'd never met anyone like Travis before.

Rafford was a small but growing town. A few years ago the business boom had struck, and the old sleepy town had begun to expand. When Sharon had been in first grade, there had been just a single class of twenty-odd kids. Now, in high school, thanks to the growth of the town there were three classes of more than thirty students each. Every year, the town grew, and new faces appeared. She guessed that Travis and his family must have moved in over the summer. It shocked her to realize he'd been at Rafford High for weeks before she'd noticed him. What had she been missing? Maybe she would soon find out. . . .

The bell rang, signaling the start of classes. It broke Sharon's dreamy mood, and she hurried along with Chiku to first period. It was strange how her mood had completely changed. The fear and brooding of last night's nightmare had vanished. In its place was a vision of deep brown eyes and a lazy smile.

They slipped into the art room and into their places, hoping not to be singled out by Mr. Levine. The teacher did look across at them, and his beard twitched slightly, but they were in luck. This was one of his good days. When he wanted to, his temper

17

could make him loud and sarcastic. Instead, he carried on with whatever it was that he had been saying, but Sharon was lost in her thoughts.

Finally he stopped talking and let them get to work. Sharon picked up her pad and charcoal and started to sketch. She had some drawing ability, though her main love was literature. She wasn't really too surprised to see a new but already fascinating face taking shape as she drew.

Mr. Levine came up as she was working, making his usual round of the room. He raised an eyebrow and scratched at what little hair remained above the level of his ears. "Not bad, Sharon," he complimented her. "I see you've met Mr. Hale, then."

Sharon felt herself blushing and glanced up. One or two of the boys sniggered and whispered to each other. The teacher's cold stare soon stopped them. Then his gaze returned to her sketch. "You're finally showing some talent here," he told her. "Though you haven't got the proportions right, around the ears. Just here." He tapped the drawing with the tool he was holding, and Sharon suddenly felt very cold.

It was a knife, identical to the one in her dream. The wooden handle, the thin neck, the widened blade. Crusted on the blade was something dried and red. . . .

THREE

"Sharon? Are you all right?" Mr. Levine asked, staring at her. "You've gone whiter than my paints." He peered down at her.

Involuntarily, Sharon flinched, shying away from the knife. She didn't dare take her eyes off it. Her sketchbook flopped onto the floor, her charcoals fell and rolled.

Puzzled, Mr. Levine raised a hand toward her, and she drew quickly back in her chair. Someone grabbed her, and Sharon cried, jerking herself free, finally snapping her gaze away from the knife. It was Chiku.

"Steady," her friend said, holding on to her this time. Sharon could feel herself shivering. Chiku looked at the art teacher. "She's not feeling too good, Mr. Levine," she explained. "Maybe I should take her to see the nurse."

Mr. Levine was clearly confused about the whole thing. "That's probably for the best," he agreed.

"You're excused." He bent to pick up the spilled art materials.

Sharon allowed Chiku to lead her outside. Once the door had closed behind them, she let out a loud sigh and tried to gather her wits. Chiku examined her critically.

"What happened to *you?*"

Sharon swallowed and walked meekly along with Chiku. "That knife he was holding."

"What about it?"

"It was the knife from my dream," she said shakily. "I know it was. It looked exactly the same as the one that I see all the time. And it had blood on it."

Chiku snorted. "That was *paint,* not blood," she said. "That's a palette knife. Artists use them when they're doing an oil painting. They use it to take the paint from the palette to the canvas. And they spread large areas of paint with it. It's not used to *cut.*"

"I don't care," Sharon insisted. "That's the knife I've been dreaming about for weeks. Say what you like, but that's the knife the man in my dream wants to kill me with." She shuddered again.

"You mean a knife like that one?"

"Not *like* it—that's the knife!" She was absolutely certain now. "I know it is. And I know it sounds crazy, but that's the knife from my dream—Mr. Levine's art knife."

Chiku stared at her, then shook her head. "I don't know what you mean," she admitted. "Sharon, it's just a dream you're having, that's all. You can't be serious about that knife being the one from the dream. You're just a bit confused. Dreams aren't *real.*"

"That's easy for you to say," Sharon snapped. "You're not the one who has this nightmare all the time."

"I guess," Chiku agreed. They had reached the nurse's office, and she knocked. When they heard a reply, she took Sharon in, explaining to the nurse that she was feeling tired and stressed out.

The nurse gave Sharon a quick examination and suggested that she rest. Then she took Chiku outside. Quietly, she asked her: "Is there anything you'd like to tell me?"

Chiku stared at the nurse, puzzled. "Like what? She's just tired."

"I'll say. From the look of her, she's missed a lot of sleep lately. Boyfriend troubles? Or is she doing anything?"

"Drugs?" Chiku laughed. "Sharon doesn't even take an aspirin when she's got a headache. She's not doing anything, believe me." Concern for her friend won out over her natural reluctance to trust any adult. "She's been having some bad dreams lately."

"Well, she's in need of rest," the nurse said flatly. "I'm going to suggest that she see her doctor." She looked perceptively at Chiku. "To her parents, of course. I doubt that the young lady will listen to me. You'd better get back to your class. I'll keep her here for a while to get some rest, then she can rejoin you."

She obviously was telling Chiku to go. The girl nodded and left. Back in her office, the nurse went to the computer records and started to hunt for Sharon's files.

Inside the small sickroom, Sharon lay on the daybed. She'd been loosely covered with a blanket and ordered to try and sleep. But that was impossible. Each time she closed her eyes, all she could see was the art knife, with something red dripping off the edges. . . . No matter how crazy it might seem, she knew that her nightmare was more than a bad dream. And that knife she had just seen was definitely the one she'd dreamed about four times. There was a slight nick in the handle that she could recall exactly from her nightmares.

She shuddered and tried again and again to dispel the image. It refused to go away.

Sharon returned to her classes later in the morning, but Chiku could see that her friend hadn't gotten any rest. She was apparently still brooding about the knife and barely paid attention in class. She was just lucky that none of the teachers seemed to have noticed her distraction. Chiku tried to talk to her several times, but Sharon simply shook her head in reply.

Finally, the end of the day arrived. As they were heading out of the door, Sharon grabbed Chiku by the arm. "I've got to check," she said determinedly.

"Check what? What are you talking about?"

"That knife." Sharon glanced in the direction of the art room. "It's been haunting me all day. Chiku, I swear I'm not crazy. But that's definitely the same knife from my dream. I just want to look at it again, and be absolutely certain."

"And then what?" Chiku sighed. "Burn it, so you'll be free of the magic spell it's cast on your dreams?"

"Chiku, be serious."

"Serious?" Chiku laughed scornfully. "Listen to yourself. You're getting paranoid about a stupid knife that's used to mix paint. And you think I'm going to take it seriously?" Then she felt bad, because she saw the hurt in her friend's eyes. "All right," she agreed reluctantly. "Let's take a look at it, if it'll make you feel better."

"I don't think that *better* is how I'll feel," Sharon admitted. "But I've got to know. I'm sorry for being such a pain."

"Hey, what are friends for?" asked Chiku. "If you can't be a pain with me, who can be?"

They made their way to the art room together. There was no one there, which made Chiku feel better. She'd rather not have any witnesses to her stupidity. They glanced about the room, but it had obviously been cleaned up. There was no sign of the knife anywhere.

"Now what?" Chiku asked Sharon. She had been hoping the knife would be sitting on Mr. Levine's desk, so they could have this over with fast. "Do we search the place?"

"Now," said Mr. Levine's voice from the doorway, "you might perhaps tell me what you're looking for?"

They spun around guiltily and saw him watching

23

them with an angry expression on his face. "If there's something you'd like, perhaps you'd be good enough to ask me? It is, after all, my room." He cocked his head to one side, waiting.

Glancing at Sharon, Chiku saw that she was completely at a loss. It was up to her, then. "I was hoping to get a look at that palette knife you were using earlier," she explained, inventing as she went along. "It's my birthday soon, and I was thinking of asking my father to buy me some paints. I figured that whatever you used would have to be the best available."

"Really?" he asked dryly.

"Cross my heart." She grinned.

He obviously wasn't certain whether or not to believe her, but he finally nodded. "It is a good model," he agreed. "But I locked it away in the supply cabinet. Hang on a moment." He took the key from his pocket and led the way across the room. Sharon followed quietly, her eyes watching his every move. If Mr. Levine noticed, he didn't remark on it.

Then he frowned. "What the blazes?" he snapped.

The cabinet had been forced open, its lock hanging loosely.

Mr. Levine wrenched open the door and peered carefully inside. "Well," he said. "There doesn't seem to be anything missing. All the supplies are in the right places."

"Maybe we scared off whoever broke in, when we came," Chiku suggested. "But there was no one here when we arrived."

"Probably just simple vandalism," the teacher

said angrily. "Some of you kids think that any lock is fair game these days."

"Not us, Mr. Levine," Chiku assured him.

"No, not you," he agreed. "But I'll have to report this. Still, while you're here . . ." His voice trailed away, and his hand stopped on the way to one of the shelves. "That's odd."

"What is?"

"There *is* something missing. That knife you were so interested in. It's gone." He turned his gaze back to them again. "If I hadn't seen you when you came in, you'd both be prime suspects. But who on earth would want to steal something like that?"

Chiku looked up and caught Sharon's haunted face. Whoever it was that had stolen the knife, it was obvious what Sharon was thinking.

The knife was now in the hands of the killer from her dreams. . . .

FOUR

As they left the school building, Chiku patted Sharon on the arm. "Relax, will you?" she asked. "It's got to be some sort of weird coincidence, that's all."

"Oh, sure," replied Sharon sarcastically. "The knife that a maniac is trying to use to kill me in my dreams is the *only* thing some thief steals from an art-supply cabinet. That's really likely."

"Oh, stop it!" Chiku had finally reached her limit. "Listen to yourself, Sharon! This is crazy! I dream about all kinds of things, but none of them come true. But you're acting like this nightmare you've been having is *real*. It can't be—it's just a bad dream, and you'll get over it. Give me a break!"

"What about the stolen knife?"

"It's just a silly coincidence. Things like that happen. It doesn't mean anything." Chiku gripped her friend's hands. "Come on. You've got to realize that it's the only sensible explanation. Spooky stuff like you're thinking just happens in those dumb movies Larry watches."

Sharon sighed. "I wish I could believe that, Chiku, honest. But I can't. You're not the one having this nightmare, always the same. It's too real for me to just dismiss it." She looked at Chiku, and there was fear in her eyes. "I know that dreams are just jumbles of memories and desires and so on. At least, almost all of them are. But this one's different. It really is. And it scares me, Chiku. I have this feeling that it's true somehow." She shuddered. "And something else has just occurred to me."

"What's that?"

"How do we know that the knife was stolen? Maybe Mr. Levine still has it. We've only got his word for it that it's missing, you know. Maybe he's still got it, and he's planning to use it."

Chiku laughed, but it sounded strained even to her ears. "What? Now you think that Levine's some kind of slasher maniac? You're sounding dumber every minute, girl."

"Am I?" Sharon asked. "Am I really?"

It wasn't a good evening for Sharon. She sat in her room and tried to concentrate on her homework, but her mind kept drifting back to the art knife, no matter what she did. She tried to conjure up Travis's face, hoping to dispel her depressed mood, but somehow she couldn't manage. With a sigh, she pushed the books to the back of her desk and glanced about the room.

The desk, the dresser, and the bedframe were all

27

wood, painted white with pink trim. When she was eleven, she had thought it was cute. Now she wished she'd picked something a little less juvenile. She still liked the canopy over the bed, though. She was glad that the old Menudo sheets were long gone, replaced with floral patterns now. She couldn't believe she'd ever liked that group! The crate of records by her stereo was filled with much better groups. She toyed with the thought of listening to something, but nothing appealed at the moment. With a sigh, she got up and examined herself in the full-length mirror.

Great. The lack of sleep was giving her bloodshot eyes. Just what she needed when she went out with Travis. Moodily, she pulled off her shirt and tossed it onto the bed. Then she dragged out a knitted green sweater and pulled it on. Maybe this for the date . . . ? No, it made her look too chunky. She tried on a loose T-shirt, then a blue blouse. Nothing seemed right. And nothing took her mind off that image of the knife, with the redness dripping . . .

Dinner was just as bad. Sharon pushed her food around with virtually no appetite at all. When she felt her mother's eyes on her, she managed to take a forkful of whatever dinner was, and routinely chewed and swallowed. But she simply couldn't concentrate.

"The nurse called me at work today," Mrs. Anders remarked in the silence. She was in her early forties and still pretty. She was in better shape than most of Sharon's friends' mothers, and her fair hair was natural. But her face was lined with concern at the moment. "She thinks you've been overdoing it a bit, Sharon. You do look tired."

Sharon shrugged. "I haven't been sleeping too well," she admitted.

"The nurse thought we should have Dr. Bryce give you a checkup," her mother added. She looked over at her husband, and he put down the legal papers he'd been looking at and nodded his agreement.

"You do look a bit run-down," he told her. "It's probably just a case of overstudying, or something. But we made you an appointment for tomorrow, just to be sure." Being a lawyer, he was ready to argue his case even with her, but Sharon didn't have the will to protest. Instead, she just nodded and stabbed at whatever was on her plate with her fork.

"Okay."

After a few more silent minutes, Mr. Anders asked, with an attempt at good humor: "So, how was school today?"

"Okay," Sharon replied. Then she remembered Travis. "Oh, is it all right if I go out on Saturday? There's a new guy in school this year, and he has tickets."

"Oh?" Her father raised an eyebrow and smiled. "To what?"

Sharon searched her memory but drew a blank. "I'm not sure," she admitted. "I'll ask him, though."

Mr. Anders laughed. "Well, as long as it's not to some head-banging rock concert, I guess it's okay." He raised a finger warningly. "But he'd better check out with us, first!"

Sharon nodded and excused herself. As she was leaving the room, she heard her father say quietly: "See, Deb? It's just boys she's got on her mind. She is sixteen, after all."

Sharon sighed. It wasn't only Travis on her mind, unfortunately. It was the missing knife. But she couldn't tell him that.

Her dark mood grew stronger as the night drew in. She worked on her essay without even being certain of the subject. Finally, she could fight back the waves of exhaustion no longer. Turning off the study light, she went downstairs to kiss her parents goodnight. They were in a cheerful mood, certain they'd discovered the reason for her quietness. She only wished that the feeling was infectious.

Upstairs, she quickly got ready for bed. Slipping on a fresh nightgown, she went to her bed, then hesitated. Glancing around the room, she saw that her closet door was still open. She frowned, certain that she had shut it earlier. A childhood memory came back to her. She had always insisted on the closet door being shut before she settled into bed. She had been convinced that some terrible monster lived inside it, and if there was even the slightest crack in the door, it would creep out in the night to devour her.

She was too old for that now, of course. But she crossed to the closet anyway and looked inside. Just in case. All she could see were her clothes and the boxes of letters, clippings, and books she kept in there. And an old stuffed doll, one of the many toys that she hadn't played with in years. There were no monsters, and no dark men with knives. Carefully, she closed the door. Then she crossed back to the bed. She was just about to climb in when she looked back and froze.

The door was open again.

Slowly, carefully, Sharon breathed in, calming down her racing heart. Her palms felt sweaty. She wiped them on her gown as she warily moved back toward the closet. There was a silence all around her as she reached out slowly to touch the handle.

Nothing. It looked just as before.

She closed the door more firmly this time, then took a couple of steps backward.

The door swung silently open once again.

Fighting back an urge to scream, Sharon gripped the door handle and swung the door shut. It felt odd, somehow. Inspecting it, she breathed out loudly. The handle was broken. It wasn't locking when she shut the door. That was all. Nothing sinister, just a broken lock. She'd mention it to her father in the morning, and he'd fix it. Glancing around her room, she saw her crate of records. It was pretty heavy, and she dragged it across to the closet. She closed the door and kicked the crate into place. That should hold it.

Then she returned to her bed and slipped between the sheets. She threw one last look at the closet, but it was—of course!—still shut. Reaching over, she clicked off the light.

Darkness settled in around her as she lay there, eyes screwed shut. She was determined not to think about the knife. Not at all. She concentrated instead on bringing Travis's face to her mind. *Think only good things!* She thought about going out with him on Saturday and enjoying herself. She kept her mind fixed on thoughts of romance. *Drive out the fear!*

Playing a game, she tried to imagine a background for him. Did he have a family? Well, obviously he must have. Parents, of course. Maybe a brother or sister? She'd always wanted a sibling herself, feeling a little lonely without a kid brother or sister to boss about, or an older one to go to for advice and stuff. So, yes, he'd have a kid . . . sister, that was it. Someone who worshiped him, wishing she could grow up like her older brother. Spinning these fantasies, she gradually relaxed.

Surprisingly quickly, she drifted off to sleep.

The alarm went off, and Sharon reached for the snooze button. She hit it on the second attempt. Enjoying the comfort of the sheets about her, she lazed away the few minutes until it sounded again. Then she turned off the clock. She hadn't had that nightmare, amazingly enough. She dimly recalled something about being stuck in an elevator with Travis, and she blushed as she remembered a few of the details. . . . Much better things to dream about! She wriggled a bit, thinking how silly it was. She'd just talked to him once, and gazed into his eyes, and here she was, imagining it was love at first sight. Or . . . maybe it was?

She rolled over, and then sat up so fast, she was dizzy for a second.

The closet door was open again, and the crate of records was about three feet from it.

Heart slamming against her ribs, Sharon threw back the covers and jumped to the carpet. Not at all sure she wanted to, she crossed to the dark mouth of the open door. How could this have happened? It couldn't have done it itself, surely?

She peered around the door and into the gloomy depths.

There was no monster, or any other figure that didn't belong. But, with a shudder that racked her entire body, Sharon's eyes were drawn to her old rag doll.

It was no longer on the shelf. Instead, it was impaled on one of the clothing hooks, pierced through its chest—in exactly the same spot that the slasher in her dreams stabbed her. And the stuffing from the doll had drained into a dark pool on the closet floor.

FIVE

"Weird stuff," Chiku muttered after hearing Sharon's latest account. She closed the door of her locker, then hit it as she struggled to get the lock back into place. "Maybe you've been sleepwalking? You know, and did that stuff to the doll yourself."

Sharon gave her a withering look. "I don't think so. I know I didn't open the closet myself. I *saw* it swing open by itself."

"Yeah, well, you said it was a bad lock, that's all."

"Maybe," Sharon agreed. "But it was fine when I changed clothes earlier yesterday. Anyway, Dad said he'd replace it when he gets home tonight. I made him promise to get one with a lock on it."

Shrugging, Chiku made a face. Pulling a small mirror from her bag, she examined herself critically. "Is my clip on straight?"

Sharon glanced at it quickly. This time it was a rose encrusted with tacky rhinestones. "Yeah." She shivered. "I'm getting spooked just going into my room at night."

"I guess that makes about as much sense as anything else you've said these past couple of weeks," Chiku replied. "Are you sure you haven't been borrowing some of Larry's videos?"

"Did I hear you mention my name?" Larry had walked up while they were preoccupied. He was smirking. "I knew you couldn't resist my charm forever."

"Right," Chiku drawled sarcastically. "Dream on, dude. It's as close as you'll ever get to me."

"Speaking of dreams," he said, smiling, not at all put off, "I just got a new video. It's called *Nighty Nightmare*. Wanna see it at my place?"

Chiku smiled as insincerely as she could manage. "Not only do I not want to see it at *your* place, I don't want to see it at *any* place."

"I love a girl who knows her own mind," Larry told her.

"And I love a guy who's *got* his own mind. Which you seem to have mislaid. Why don't you go look for it and leave me alone?"

Larry grinned again. "Ah, you're just playing hard to get. See you around."

"I never go around," Chiku called after him, then turned a happy face toward Sharon. "See? I told you he was crazy about me."

"Keep this up, and he'll just be annoyed with you." Sharon sighed. "And I'm getting worried that maybe I'm just going crazy."

"Hey, don't talk like that." Chiku frowned at her

friend. "You're as sane as the next person. Provided," she added with an impish expression, "that the next person is me, of course."

Sharon looked up, but bit back whatever she was going to say. Chiku glanced around and saw Travis approaching them. He was dressed in a brown sweatshirt that almost perfectly matched his eyes. He waved and called: "Still on for Saturday?"

Her heart feeling considerably lighter, Sharon nodded. "My parents said it's fine, as long as it's not to a heavy-metal concert. They're kind of old-fashioned." Sharon shrugged, embarrassed. "They think that all rock stars are inspired by the devil, or something."

"Well, aren't they?" he teased. "No, it's not heavy-metal. Look, maybe I could stop by and take you for a soda later? It would give them a chance to check me out. I know parents like that stuff. This way they can be happy that I haven't got three heads, or a van. Unless they're into three heads and vans?"

"Not that I know of." Despite her earlier fears, Sharon had to laugh. Travis was so up that she couldn't stay depressed. And, unlike most of the guys she'd dated, he actually didn't seem to mind meeting her folks. "That sounds good. About what time?"

"Eightish?" he suggested. "I wouldn't want to interrupt dinner."

"Fine." She smiled at him. "See you tonight."

"Count on it." He flashed her his own grin, then nodded to Chiku. "Are you sure your parents named you right? You haven't been chattering much."

"A chance to get a few words in would be nice," she told him. "But I know when I'm intruding."

He laughed. "Good. I'll keep that in mind when I want to be alone with Sharon."

Chiku dug her elbow in Sharon's ribs. "If you ever get tired of him, I get first refusal, right?"

"What about Larry?"

Raising her chin proudly, Chiku replied: "Think I can't handle two guys at once?"

Still giggling, they headed for their first class. Sharon felt almost drunk with the simple normalcy of the whole thing. It was wonderful just to worry about what her parents would think of Travis, instead of being haunted by crazy people with knives.

After school, Sharon went to her appointment with Dr. Bryce. After the inevitable wait, he called her in. As usual, he dispensed with idle conversation and subjected her to a swift but thorough examination. Finally, he started to make notes and glanced up at her.

"Well, how do you feel? Any obvious problems?"

She shook her head. "I just can't seem to get enough sleep."

"So your mother mentioned." He tapped his pencil thoughtfully against his lower teeth. "Well, you'll be relieved to hear that there seems to be nothing physically wrong with you. I had expected anemia. A lot of you young girls diet to stay slender and miss out on a lot of essential vitamins. But you seem fine there—though I'll have to wait for the blood test results before I can positively clear you. Still, your reflexes are fine, and you seem in good shape." Then he pierced her with a look. "Bad dreams?"

How did he know? Almost as if she'd been caught stealing, she flushed, then nodded.

He seemed to have expected it. "It's not uncommon," he told her. "You're at an age where many things are difficult for you. School pressures, exams, grades, and so on. Choosing your career, the direction for the rest of your life. Well, I'll write you a prescription for a mild tranquilizer. You don't *have* to take them—but if you're really having trouble sleeping, they might just help." He handed her the sheet, and with it a business card. "That's for a therapist I know who's very good. If you persist with these troubling dreams, you might want to see her. She can help you get to the root of the problem if it becomes necessary."

Sharon glanced at the card, noting the name Dr. Helena Jablonski. Nodding, she placed it and the prescription in her bag. "Thank you." Then she left, glad it was over. She could fill the prescription in the shopping center and call her mother from there to pick her up. She hadn't really expected the doctor to be much use, but the pills might help some.

Anyway, enough of that! Travis was coming over tonight, and she still had to decide what to wear. . . .

"All done," her father said, placing the screwdriver back in his tool kit and straightening up. He looked at the new closet handle with pride. "Better than ever," he told her.

"Thanks, Dad," she replied. "You don't know how much I appreciate this." *Especially since I can lock this one.*

"No problem. What else are fathers for?"

"Kissing," she told him, and gave him one on the cheek.

He smiled. "Better get ready. This fellow of yours will be here any time." He glanced at the old lock in his hand. "Shoddy workmanship, that's all it is. They don't make things the way they used to." Then he smiled again. "Words fathers have told their children for thousands of years, no doubt."

"Probably." She laughed, loving the way he never seemed to take himself too seriously. He might be one of the best lawyers in the state, but he never let it go to his head. "Now, if you'd be so kind as to leave? I haven't changed in front of you since I was seven."

"Six," he corrected her with a mock frown. "You were an early developer." With a wink, he left, closing the door.

She glanced at the clock. The red numbers showed 6:32.

Grief! She'd better get a move on!

Downstairs again, Mr. Anders replaced his tool kit in the garage. He glanced up from his neat workbench to see his wife looking worriedly at him. With a reassuring smile, he crossed to her, putting his arm about her shoulders.

After a moment, she voiced her thoughts: "Why does Sharon want a closet door she can lock?"

He shrugged. "She's sixteen—who knows *what's* going through her mind? She probably just wants somewhere she can keep all those secret things teenagers think their parents never had when they were kids."

"I don't know," his wife answered. "She's been acting awfully funny lately. She seems so tired all the time, and she's even been a bit short with me, which isn't like her."

Mr. Anders snorted good-humoredly. "It's just her age," he assured her. "She's got a new boyfriend, grades to watch, and her entire adult life to worry about. Sixteen-year-olds do funny things." He glanced at the broken lock he was still holding in his free hand. "This thing breaking gave her an excuse to get a place to hide all her little secrets. It'll make her feel better, you mark my words. After all, what can she have that she'd want to hide from us?"

Mrs. Anders still looked worried. "Nothing as serious as what we're hiding from her." Her eyes were haunted.

SIX

Sharon sat in front of her mirror, lazily brushing her long, blond hair. The evening had been filled with nerve-wracking moments and dizzying highs. She was still almost flying, humming gently to herself with each stroke of the brush.

Her parents had taken to Travis from the start, and he had been polite, but not quiet. It turned out that he was another passionate viewer of *L.A. Law*, which instantly won over her mother. And he had a slightly battered Thunderbird, a car her father had always liked. (She suspected that her father would have approved of anything except a van with wall-to-wall carpeting!) And the tickets he had were for a concert—but not rock. It was for a folk group, and he explained apologetically that he liked the quieter stuff.

That had convinced the Anderses he was perfect.

He had taken Sharon out for a soda, promising she'd be back within two hours (which he had meticulously checked against his watch throughout the evening). Thankful that her parents hadn't embarrassed her too much with pointed questions, Sharon had been on edge, wondering what he thought of her folks and her house. He assured her that he had liked both, and she was relieved. He complimented her outfit—after a lot of insecurity, she'd elected to go with the casual look and wore her green pants and a soft gold top. All in all, he was gently perfect.

Sharon had expected that they'd go to the Golden Mall, where most of the kids from school hung out. She'd looked forward to being seen with Travis, imagining the envy of the other girls. Apart from Chiku, she hadn't really seen much of her usual crowd of friends lately. They had gotten tired of her edginess and occasional outbursts of anger— not aimed at them, but not appreciated, either. Sharon had delicious visions of turning their heads by arriving with her prize date.

Instead, Travis had taken her to one of the newer shopping centers out closer to where he lived. The small café there was new, but very pleasant. A little disappointed that there was no one there she knew and could impress, Sharon buried her feelings and concentrated on enjoying her evening. Travis had gently asked questions, and she had gushed quite shamelessly, happy to tell him what she could—her plans to attend college, to become a teacher, all about her early life. . . . She skirted around plans of romance coyly, and he let the hints lie dormant. She told him about Chiku, who'd been her best

42

friend for five years, and even boldly suggested that maybe she and Travis could double-date with Chiku and Larry. Travis had sidestepped the question, pointing out that Chiku hadn't even agreed to see Larry yet. Sharon got a clear impression that Travis didn't like Larry too much, though he didn't say anything against him.

In fact, Travis didn't say much at all. He was quite happy, it seemed, to let her talk. She caught him looking at her with those deep brown eyes several times, and was furious that each time she blushed like some silly kid on a first date. Which, in many ways, was how she felt. Insecurely, she even excused herself twice to go to the bathroom and check on her makeup. She wanted so badly for everything to be perfect! She thought she looked okay, but did he?

Finally, he had announced that they had better be heading back before her parents started calling the police. He had dropped her off, politely saying good-night to her folks and promising to talk to Sharon in the morning at school. After he had gone, her parents had complimented her taste.

Sharon was still on an emotional high now. With a satisfied sigh, she replaced the hairbrush on her armoire and slipped out of her robe. She caught sight of herself in the mirror, her fair hair setting off the dusty blue flimsiness of her nightgown. She wondered how Travis would like to see her in this. . . . Then she bit back the thoughts that were threatening to break past her defenses. She'd only been out with him on one very short date!

She crossed to the bed and then looked up at the closet door.

It was still closed. Determinedly, she walked over and locked it, placing the key next to her brush on the dresser. Satisfied now, she returned to her bed and slipped under the sheets. Finally, she switched off the light and pulled the sheets up. Wriggling around a bit, she found a comfortable position and let her mind drift. . . .

The darkness was complete.

Sharon stood bewildered for a moment. All she could hear was the faint sound of her own breathing. She could feel sand or soil under her bare feet. There was a slight breeze, nipping icily at her bare legs.

The dream again!

Her heart started to speed up, and she looked around wildly. Her right hand came up and caught against a branch. She was in the woods, as always. It was beginning. . . .

It was always the same. She always knew that she was dreaming, but that didn't stop her terror. She moved her foot, slowly, and could feel the ice-cold stones that lay on the ground, waiting to trip her as she ran.

She wouldn't run. Not this time. This time, she'd be strong, this time she'd—

But she always thought that. And she always ran. She couldn't help it.

The breeze ruffled her nightgown, like some chill lover. She could feel goose bumps all over her skin, and shuddered. If only she could be dressed warmer when she had this dream! But she always wore whatever she had fallen asleep in.

Maybe she'd better buy some thicker nightgowns!

This attempt at humor fell flat. The panic was starting already. Each beat of her heart seemed faster, stronger, and louder than the one before it. Blood pounded in her ears. Her palms started to sweat. Something began to beat in her mind, compelling her to start running.

No! She wouldn't! Not this time, not—

Terror fastened onto her like some sickening cloak. She stumbled, almost to her knees, and then she ran.

The darkness wasn't total after all. She could make out vague, grotesque forms. Stunted, dead skeletons of trees, with bony arms and fingers trying to claw her hair and eyes. Throwing out her right arm, she tried to protect herself. The wood scratched at her skin, leaving welts and droplets of blood.

In the distance, there was a cry. Some animal or bird in terrible pain, it rose and fell, then choked off abruptly. Skidding to a halt, Sharon desperately looked around, but could see nothing except the damp blackness of the ground and the ugly, twisted shapes of the trees. Then came the sound of beating wings as something swooped at her.

Flinging her hands up, Sharon gave a startled cry. Something hurtled out of the night and thudded against her left arm. She had a vague sensation of something leathery, then with a smack from the unseen wings, the creature rose again into the air. She could feel the down-draft from the loudly flapping wings, and then it was back.

Tiny sharp teeth fastened onto her arm, ripping into the skin. A tongue rasped across the open wound, lapping at her blood. The weight of the creature made Sharon stagger, and she screamed in pain and terror. With her right hand, she hit outward, toward the snuffling sounds of the thing and the pain in her arm. She connected with something, and hit it again. With a cry of indignation, whatever it was whirled into the air.

Sharon doubled over and ran again, sucking in every bit of air she could manage. Her left forearm was a mass of pain, and she could feel the blood seeping from the open wound. It would need fixing, but first she had to get away.

After terrifying moments, she stopped and just missed colliding into one of the misshapen trees. Chest heaving, heart pounding, she listened, but there was no sound of wings. She had escaped it! Feverishly, not knowing how long she had to spare, she ripped at her nightgown hem, tearing free a strip about two feet long. Breathing in short, loud gasps, she leaned against a tree and worked on tying the strip of cloth about her wound as best she could. It wasn't the best job of bandaging she'd ever done, but it would have to do for now.

Then it hit her: *This wasn't how the dream went! It had changed!*

For the first time, the dream had shifted. Once,

46

she would have bet that any change had to be for the better, but not now.

This dream was worse than the old ones. Much worse.

Sharon stared wildly out into the darkness. Nothing. Then, from above, something dropped onto her bare shoulder. Something small, many-legged, chittering. Sharon screamed again, turning her head away and brushing at it frantically. The insect-thing lost its grip on her sweaty skin, but fell into the neckline of her nightgown. Hysterically, Sharon slapped at herself, her skin crawling at the feel of the thing, until it finally fell out. Wildly, she ran again; anything, just to get away.

She felt wretched, dirty, and filled with pain. Lungs consumed with fire, she ran and ran until her strength was gone and she simply couldn't run any further. Weak, nauseated, and tired beyond belief, she finally slumped to the cold, wet ground, her every breath racking her body with agony. Things didn't look black now—they had a red sheen over them, caused by the pain in her eyes. Her head was spinning and her left arm burned. Maybe whatever had bit her had poisoned her?

If so, she hoped it worked fast. Anything to escape this misery.

She pushed herself into a sitting position and stared back into the blackness she had run from.

They were there. She knew it. The man and the not-man, the watcher. They were there, and they were ready, now that she was too tired, too emotionally drained to fight back.

The man stepped out of the shadows. As always, she could make him out quite clearly, despite the lack of light. The dark features, the long, dirty hair, the sick smile, the burning eyes—and the art knife he carried. There was something nudging the edge of her mind, something that suggested she knew him somehow. But the thought never gelled. She stared at him, then her eyes focused on the ever-present palette knife.

This time, though, the knife was dripping red, leaving a trail as the man slowly walked toward her. *Blood or paint?* she wondered. Did it matter?

Sharon whimpered in fear and tried to shuffle away from the relentless approach. It seemed to amuse her tormentor. His smile grew wider and more demonic.

"There's no escape, Sharon," he hissed, raising the knife slightly. "Not now. Not ever."

"Why are you doing this to me?" she choked out, fascinated by the sparkling red of the blade.

"Because you're mine," the man answered.

For the first time, the un-man spoke. It was there, still unseen, unseeable. A low, whispering, hypnotic voice, barely human. "No," it sighed. "Because you're *mine.*"

Sharon didn't know why, but this terrified her more than anything had so far. That red-dripping knife was something real, something obvious to fear. The madman with the blazing eyes was solid, there. But this un-man, this voice, this whisper in the blankness—it sent a shiver not merely through her body, but through her soul, into the deepest fiber of her being.

The watcher was worse than death. Death, however horrible and painful, would at least have some end. But the voice of the watcher suggested nightmares and agonies that could never stop, that she would never be free of.

The man loomed over her, and she looked without hope of mercy into his eyes. And, for the first time, she saw something else there—beyond the fury, beyond the hatred, beyond the determination to slay her. She saw *fear* there—fear that consumed him even more than these nightmares ate at her.

He was even more haunted than she was!

And she saw that he knew what she had seen. With a cry of rage, he leaped upon her, slashing down with the knife. She felt his cold, oppressive embrace as he enfolded her, and she screamed as the knife plunged down—

—and tried to sit up. But she couldn't. She was still in darkness, wrapped in something heavy, dragging her down, pinning her. Screaming, she struggled to get free, arms and legs thrashing. Her mouth was covered in something that clung to her face, cutting off her breathing. She tried to draw in more air, but all she got was a mouthful of the covering. Choking, she couldn't even scream.

Suddenly, there was a light, then noise. She was dying, she knew. This was it—the roaring in her ears was the final marker. She felt giddy, and then suddenly she could breathe again. With deep, body-racking breaths, she sucked air into her tortured lungs and sat up in bed.

As her vision steadied, the red blur cleared, and she saw that she was in her own bed, the sheets scattered around her. Both her parents were there, looking worriedly at her. As she whooped in as much air as she could, she struggled to make some sense of what had happened—what was happening right now. The bed was covered with some blue material, and it spilled onto the floor where her father had wrenched it free of her. He held a wooden post in his hands and looked furiously at the head of her bed.

"That damned canopy," he snarled. "It must have fallen on you when you were sleeping. Thank God you felt it and started screaming. It almost smothered you."

It was beginning to make sense now, of sorts. As her breathing steadied, she looked around and saw that he was right. The posts holding up the canopy seemed to have broken, and the fabric of the canopy had covered her. That was what had woken her from the nightmare, and almost killed her in real life.

Her father was examining the stumps of the post. He swore in disgust. "Look at that," he complained. "The bolts are sheared clean through. More of that faulty workmanship, I'm afraid."

Sharon followed his gaze and saw the brightness where the metal bolts had literally split apart. The wood around it was splintered, sticking out at crazy angles. "It looks," she said hoarsely, "it looks like something *clawed* the post apart." She could still recall the un-man from her nightmare. Had it been *him*?

"Nonsense," her father said. "The wood must have split when the canopy collapsed, that's all." He snorted. "It'd take a mountain lion to do that sort of damage with claws, Sharon, and there aren't any in this neighborhood. It's too exclusive." He gave a weak laugh.

Her mother had been silent long enough. "Henry, that's enough for now. You clean up this bed so she can get back to sleep, and we'll look into repairing it in the morning." Sharon looked at her clock and saw that it was a little after 1:30. "Meanwhile," her mother continued, "I'm going to see to Sharon. Some of that splintered wood must have cut her."

Now that her mother had mentioned it, Sharon realized that her arm was hurting her badly. Her left arm, where that creature had bitten her in the dream. She looked down at it dully.

There was a mass of semi-dried blood in exactly the same spot. But no bandage.

"If the wood cut me," she said slowly, slurring her words tiredly together, "then how come it's already starting to scab?" She felt light-headed, but she couldn't be certain whether it was from loss of blood or because she was coming down from the adrenaline high caused by her fear.

"Don't worry about it," her mother told her. "I'll help you clean it up. Come on."

Her father started cleaning up the mess of the collapsed canopy as Sharon swung her feet out of bed. Mrs. Anders helped her to the bathroom and sat her down. She gathered together antiseptic, bandages, and aspirin, then started to work on the injured arm. Sharon concentrated on simply breathing and calming down. It had been a night that had ripped her nerves almost raw.

"That's odd," her mother muttered. "Why didn't you tell me you'd torn this nightgown?"

Sharon looked down and saw that a strip of material had been torn off the bottom of the light gown. The same amount she'd ripped off in her dream to make the bandage. But that hadn't been on her arm.

She looked up and realized that her mother was still waiting for a reply. "I—I just forgot," she said lamely.

"Well, you'd better remember when we go shopping. You're going to have to trash that one." She patted Sharon on the shoulder. "Is that better?"

Testing the feel of the bandaged arm, Sharon nodded gratefully. "Much."

"Good. Let's see if your father's made your room presentable again. Do you need help to stand?"

Sharon shook her head and managed to clamber to her feet again. She felt drained, but the pain was mostly gone now. And the fear had ebbed to a tolerable level. She realized that her mother was handing her two more tablets, and she swallowed them before she thought to ask what they were.

"Dr. Bryce's tranquilizers," her mother answered. "They should help you catch up on the lost sleep."

Nodding, Sharon managed to make it back to her room. Her father had done a good job, and the bed looked presentable again. He had returned to his own bed. Sharon smiled at her mother thinly.

"I'll be all right," she assured her. "You'd better get back to sleep yourself."

Her mother smiled and stroked her hair. "Get your rest," she said, and then left.

Sharon closed her door and leaned against it, staring at her bed. It looked fine now, but incomplete without the canopy, naturally. It should be safe to get back in it. She couldn't accept her father's idea that the supports had just collapsed somehow. And she still thought that the wood splinters looked like a giant claw had slashed at the wood, bringing the overhead material crashing down onto her.

Claws belonging to that shape in the night? Sharon shuddered at the thought. That monster was just something in her dream, wasn't it? It wasn't real, surely? But—that wound in her arm had happened in the dream, and the tear in her nightie—both turned out to be very real.

She was beginning to feel drowsy again, undoubtedly the pills kicking in. She started to go to her bed when a glint of metal caught her eye. She turned to look down at the carpet and saw the key to the closet there.

But she had put the key on the dresser when she went to bed. It was six feet away from there now. How could it have gotten here? Maybe her father had caught it with something when he took out the ruins of the canopy?

But wouldn't that have dragged the key toward the doorway to the hall? This was in exactly the opposite direction. As if it had been trying to crawl across the carpet toward the closet. . . .

Sharon picked the key up. Then, driven by an impulse she couldn't explain, she hurriedly crossed to the closet and unlocked the door. She opened it carefully, but there was no sign of movement. She was about to shut and lock it again when she saw something and stiffened in shock.

Now she knew where the missing strip from her nightgown had gone. It was in here, hanging from the same hook that the doll had been impaled on. And the other end of the strip was wrapped about the neck of an old Barbie doll. Someone had hung the doll in a noose.

Inside a locked closet.

Fighting back the chills she felt, Sharon shut the door and locked it. Then she went back to bed and thrust the key under her pillow. She slid back into bed and pulled the sheets over her. Reaching for the light, she suddenly wavered. No.

For the first time since her childhood, she went to sleep with the light on.

SEVEN

At school the next day, Sharon was nervous and irritable. Chiku, studying her thoughtfully, put up with the mood as long as she could, but finally during lunch break she probed for an explanation. It didn't take much prompting for Sharon to start talking about the events of the night.

"I don't know what frightens me the most," she concluded shakily. "The fact that things seem to be happening in real life now to match the dream, or the fact that the dream has changed. It was bad enough before, but last night really got to me."

Chiku stared at the playing field for a while before saying: "If anybody but you told me all that, I'd think they were either joking or completely nuts." She sighed and shook her head. "It sounds crazy to me, though. What have you told your parents?"

"As much as I can. That I'm having bad dreams, and they scare me."

"What did they say?"

Sharon grimaced. "They want me to go and see this therapist person my doctor recommended. They think it's all in my head, and that the bed and the closet door just broke accidentally. And that somehow the doll just fell off the shelf onto the hook. They're big believers in coincidence."

"And you're not."

"After a while," Sharon replied, "it gets to be too silly to keep calling things coincidental, doesn't it?"

"Yeah." Chiku turned a serious face to her friend. "Okay, just for the sake of argument, let's assume that you're right—that there is some connection between your dreams and these spooky things that are happening to you. Then there has to be a reason. I mean, even the supernatural has to have some sort of logic to it, doesn't it? So—any idea who this guy in the dream is, or why he's got it in for you?"

Sharon shook her head. "I've never seen him before, but he's always the same. He wears jeans and a dirty sweatshirt, and carries the knife."

"Hmm. And you always wear something different in your dreams?"

"Not exactly. I'm always wearing whatever I fell asleep in. Sometimes it's the same nightgown as the night before, of course. But always what I wore to bed." She laughed, unconvincingly. "I guess that's why it seems so real to me. But this was the first time that I woke up and what had happened in my dream had happened for real, too."

"The cut and the torn nightgown?" Chiku rubbed her chin thoughtfully. "I'll tell you something. Since you started worrying about this dream,

56

I've been doing some reading up in Dad's library about dreams. Part of his collection on folklore and mythology. You remember them?"

"Yeah. And?"

Chiku smiled grimly. She'd told Sharon years ago that she aimed to be a psychologist some day, and loved any excuse to practice her talents in the field. "Well, modern psychology thinks that they're actually the brain sort of working through and sorting out the experiences we've had in the day. Different schools of psychology disagree on whether the dreams are all based in sex, or power, or whatever. Anyway, there are two things that strike me as being related to your dream.

"First, there's this gonzo theory that despite the apparent length of time the dream lasts, they are actually formed in the mind just as we wake up, and take into account some of the things around us. Like, say, we dream about bells, and wake up and the alarm clock's going off. Well, maybe you dreamed about that vampire-whatsit attacking you and being enveloped in something because, just as you were waking up, the canopy collapsed, hurting you and trapping you."

Sharon sniffed in disbelief. "Come off it."

"Hey, I'm just telling you what I read. I don't make this stuff up!" protested Chiku. "Anyway, the other thing I read is that sometimes dreams do actually come true. Apparently both President Lincoln and President Kennedy had dreams about their own assassinations, and there are other cases of things like that happening. Sometimes, though, the dreams are just warnings of what might happen, to get us to change our behavior."

"Well, that's a great help," Sharon replied sarcastically. "In that case, I'm either going to be killed by a slasher, or else it's telling me to steer clear of woods at night in my lingerie."

"Don't get so sensitive," Chiku said. "I'm just trying to help get things straight. And there is another possibility." She looked a little embarrassed, but plunged on. "The Bible is full of stories about people seeing things in dreams. Sometimes visions, sometimes just warnings. And most cultures in the world have the same belief—that the supernatural can invade our dreams easily because our mental defenses are down. If there are such things as ghosts, or spooks, or whatever, maybe it's easier for them to contact you through your dreams than face-to-face."

"Ghosts?" Sharon frowned. "I didn't say anything about ghosts."

"I know. But maybe your house is haunted by someone who was killed there, and you've somehow tuned in to her thoughts, and you're reliving her experiences in your dreams? That way, it'd explain why you dream of death in the same way all the time."

"But the dream last night was different."

Chiku shrugged. "That's the weak spot in my great theory."

Sharon thought about it, then shook her head. "No, I don't think it's the answer. I definitely get the impression that it's *me* that the man and the thing are after. But I don't know why." Then she remembered the voice from the dream. "Wait a minute, the thing I never see said something about me belonging to it."

"Belonging to it?"

"Right." Sharon thought hard. "The slasher said something about me being his, and then the voice of the thing said that wasn't true, that I was *his*. Whatever that means."

Chiku pulled a face. "You know, the more I get to know about this dream, the creepier it sounds. And the less sense it makes. I guess I'd better do some more reading up, and see what I can find."

Sharon touched her friend's arm. "Thanks, Chiku. I really appreciate your concern. And that you believe me."

"I'm not sure about that part," Chiku answered. "Frankly, dudette, if I *really* believed you, I think I'd freak out. Oh-oh. Speaking of freaking out . . ." She nodded. Sharon followed her gaze and saw Larry waving to them.

"Don't tell me," Chiku said as he came over. "You've got a new tape that you want me to see."

"You're catching on quick." He grinned. "This is a classic—*I Ate Your Guts.*"

Chiku snorted. "Obviously a touching love story. I'll pass."

Larry shrugged. "Suit yourself. You're missing a treat."

"Doesn't sound like my taste, kid," Chiku said with a grin. "I couldn't get my teeth into it."

Sharon had to smile. "What is this? A bad-pun contest?"

"Could be." Larry laughed. "I'll bite. Bite, buy it
. . . Get it?"

Chiku raised one foot off the ground. "You'll get
something if you don't get moving," she warned.

Larry leered rather obviously at this. "And we
haven't even dated yet. I knew you'd find my charm
irresistible."

"The only thing that I find irresistible," Chiku
replied, "is the thought of kicking you hard, right up
your asteroid."

Larry backed off, grinning. Chiku shook her
head, chuckling to herself. "That boy is certifiable.
And cute. I just wish he'd ask me out to something a
bit more interesting. Like the dance." Then, checking the books she'd collected earlier from her locker,
she said: "Hell—I forgot my history book. Back in a
second." She shot off back down the corridor.
Sharon shrugged; typical Chiku, always forgetting
something.

"Does your friend really like that creep
Wauchop?"

Sharon spun around to see a vaguely familiar face.
Jenn something. She was in Larry's class, and had
always seemed like a long streak of misery to Sharon.
Shrugging, Sharon answered: "Chiku kind of likes
him, yes. Why? What's wrong with him?"

Jenn pulled a face and huddled closer, secretively.
"Lonny Petersen told me all about him. Pretty sick,
if you ask me."

Sharon thought back, but didn't recall any connection between Larry and Lonny ever being mentioned. "What does she know?"

"Well, she lives just a few doors down from him. Anyway, one night about a year ago, she was getting ready for bed and happened to look out of her window. And he was there, watching her strip." Jenn smiled in a confidential fashion. "He's a Peeping Tom."

"And she's a tramp," Sharon said, annoyed. "Getting undressed with the shades open. She just wants attention. I've heard about the stuff she gets up to. She's got a nerve talking about other people."

Annoyed that her news hadn't caused more trouble, Jenn shrugged. "Suit yourself, Anders. I was just trying to be helpful."

"Yeah—like the iceberg was trying to help the *Titanic*. Thanks a lot."

Sniffing angrily, Jenn flounced off. Burning, Sharon glared after her. *Trying to stir up trouble with that stupid story . . .*

Then, suddenly, Sharon had a terrible thought. *What if it was true? What if Larry really got his kicks watching girls undress? Or worse?* In the nightmare last night, she'd felt that there was something familiar about her attacker. Could it be that somehow it was Larry?

"Hey, Sharon," Chiku said, returning with her arms even more laden. "I think that this whole business of carting our books around is just another school plot to try to keep us in shape. If you ask me—" She broke off as she saw the haunted expression on Sharon's face. "What's wrong with you?"

"It's what you mentioned earlier," Sharon answered in a hushed voice. "About there having to be

61

a reason for whatever happens. Some sort of connection."

"So? Enlighten me."

Sharon nodded slowly in the direction that Larry had taken. "Well, I've been dreaming about some slasher trying to kill me. And I only know one person who's into that sort of film and stuff. . . ."

"Larry?" Chiku laughed. "You can't seriously think he might have anything to do with your dreams?"

"Maybe not," Sharon agreed. "But—well, he *is* into blood and gore, and all kinds of gross stuff. Maybe watching it on the screen isn't enough for him anymore?" She considered mentioning the news Jenn had told her, but rejected it. Chiku didn't need to hear that, especially since there was no proof it had even happened.

Chiku glanced nervously at her friend. "Come on," she said, shivering. "You're not serious, are you?"

"I don't know. I really don't know." Sharon stared off, trying to make some kind of logic out of the whole thing. "But I can't get the possibility out of my mind."

EIGHT

The remainder of the week passed quietly enough. It seemed almost as though the dream and the bizarre experiences had completely vanished as mysteriously as they had arrived. Sharon managed to get two nights of much-needed rest.

Then came her date with Travis. Sharon's excitement had been building up for this over the past few days. She was desperately afraid that it would turn out to be a bust and ruin all her fantasies. However, it was better than she had even hoped. Travis had shown up on time, and the club he took her to turned out to be lively and well-filled. Though the idea of hearing a folk group had sounded boring, and Sharon had been picturing something like an Appalachian jug band, the concert was a great success. The group had sung a mixture of material—some sad, some funny, some with a good beat, and even a medley of Irish pub songs that had the whole audience laughing along and joining in the rowdy choruses.

Travis had seemed completely absorbed by the music. His dark eyes had stirred, giving a hint of great depth to his thoughts. Sharon suspected that he was on some other plane of existence, very different from the cheerful club his body was in. He caught her studying him, and a slow, shared-secret smile flickered across his lips.

"Enjoying yourself?" Sharon teased him.

"More than you can imagine," Travis told her, and squeezed her hand.

I don't know, she thought to herself. *I've got a pretty vivid imagination. And if you feel anything like I feel . . .*

It was weird, totally weird. She'd dated plenty of guys before—generally in groups, but enough alone —and she'd never felt like this with any of them. She'd read her share of the slushy, unbelievable romance novels that were so popular. Their claims of instant, undying love had always seemed farfetched and stupid before. But with Travis, she suddenly found her mind changing. It felt so right being here with him, listening to this group pounding away. She was totally at peace with herself and the world. And when he turned those brown eyes on her, it was like he was seeing right into her soul.

Not bedroom eyes, exactly. With Travis it was different. His glances—especially when they lingered— set a fire burning inside her. There was the unmistakable *you fascinate me* in them, but this wasn't simply a physical thing. It was as if they were soul mates, somehow, two sides of one being. A week ago, she'd have laughed herself stupid at the idea. Now . . .

Yes, Travis was almost perfect. As he had promised her folks, he had her home just after eleven. Sharon was hoping he'd try for a kiss, and he did, of sorts. He held her hand and kissed her fingertips. She had laughed breathlessly, so he'd followed this by kissing each finger in turn. Then he had waved good-bye and driven off.

In this euphoric, vaguely unreal state of mind, Sharon got ready for bed. She found herself humming snatches from the songs she'd heard, and she felt happier than she had in months. It had been a fantastic evening, and she was certain Travis would ask her out again soon. Turning out the light, Sharon snuggled happily down beneath the covers and let her mind drift off. . . .

She was in a room of some kind, a long, tall room, well-lit. There were groups of people walking around, muttering quietly and pointing. She followed along with the crowd and saw that there were paintings on all of the walls.

She was in an art gallery of some sort, obviously. The first painting she stopped at was of something that looked very medieval. It was a knight, spearing a dragon from horseback. The dragon was trying to devour the knight, and in the background, chained to a rock, was a woman in a medieval robe, looking terrified. As she examined the painting closer, Sharon realized that the woman looked just like her, and the knight—who wore a helmet but no faceplate—was Travis. Her knight in shining armor, to the rescue! She smiled at the thought.

Then the picture began to shift, to change. The dragon moved, its claws reaching out to shatter the lance being used to attack it. The talons came down onto the knight, piercing the armor and transfixing Travis. His face twisted in pain, and both the painted Sharon and the dream Sharon were screaming in horror.

She realized then that she was alone in the gallery, and the crowds had all moved on. An unsettling itch began at the back of her mind. The painting froze into place again, but this time the scene was very different. The dragon had twisted around. Its right foot had impaled the dead knight and was standing on his body. The left foot was reaching toward the screaming woman chained to the rocks.

Sharon shuddered and turned away from the grotesque painting. She wouldn't look at it! Instead, she forced her feet to take her to the next one.

This seemed to be a Picasso or something like that. It showed what was clearly supposed to be some kind of winged figure, perhaps an angel. But it was all cubist in style—the eyes were on the same side of the face, the angles were harsh, the colors all wrong. The wings looked shredded and unable to bear the figure through the air. Everything about it was twisted. The tooth-filled mouth suddenly opened, and the eyes fixed on her own.

"Hello, Sharon."

It was the voice of the un-man, the watcher from her nightmare wood!

With a stifled cry, she turned away from the painting and found her gaze locked onto a third.

This was obviously some kind of abstract pop art. It was all shapes and lines and slashlike strokes. The predominant color was a bright blood red. There were black streaks, as if someone had taken a knife to try and destroy the painting. It was a disturbing picture, one that frightened and confused her. And, as Sharon watched, it too began to change.

The redness started to move, to pool and begin to drip from the picture's bottom edge. Against her will, Sharon held out her fingers, and the redness dripped onto her.

It wasn't paint.

She cried out, shaking with fear, trying to wipe the blood off on her nightgown. Somewhere, there was a voice laughing at her, and she felt herself falling. Giddily, she collapsed under the abstract painting, her back against the wall. The rest of the gallery was all blurred and unfocused, like she was seeing it through a kaleidoscope. She could feel blood from the painting dripping onto her skin, warm and wet. Terrified, she looked upward, and it was as if she was suddenly standing beneath a waterfall—a waterfall of blood.

Shaking in horror, screaming, she—

—sat upright in bed, covering her head and shivering.

Gradually, Sharon managed to calm herself down, taking long, deep breaths until the panic was no longer a fire but simply burning embers. Shivering, she reached for a drink of water and then froze.

She wasn't alone.

Despite the fact that the clock read 2:17, her room was never entirely dark. Stray light from outside made it possible to see shades of black and dark gray. Nervously, Sharon examined every inch she could, trying to make out whatever might be out of place. Everything seemed to be perfectly normal, except for that icy certainty that she wasn't alone. Then she saw it.

The closet door was open again.

The blackness was intense there. Not just a lack of light, but as if it were draining the light from all about her, sucking it into the maw of the closet. And the warmth with it.

In the blackness, two red eyes gleamed, studying her intently.

Sharon started shaking and couldn't get control of herself. Her throat was hoarse and silent. For several seconds—minutes?—she sat, quivering, as the red eyes looked her over.

Then something brushed against her and the immobility was gone. She threw herself from the bed, screaming, and ran to the closet door, slamming it closed on the whatever-it-was within. She was still holding the door closed when her parents burst in, flicking on the light.

"Sharon!" her mother exclaimed. "Whatever is the matter?"

"It's in there," Sharon whispered, her voice shaking. She backed away from the closet door. "The nightmare thing. It's in my closet."

Her father, still struggling to pull his bathrobe on, snorted. "You were dreaming."

She shook her head. "No. No, I wasn't. I was awake, and there were two eyes in there, staring at me."

"Well, we'll soon see about that." Mr. Anders pushed past her and tried the door.

It was locked.

He looked at Sharon, obviously in danger of losing his patience. "How could you see anything there? You just had another bad dream, that's all."

"I saw something," she insisted. "And I felt something touch me."

"She might be right about that, Henry," her mother said, pointing to the window. "Look at that."

The window was ajar by about six inches. Below it, on the floor, was some dirt. Her father crossed to examine it. "Claw marks on the sill," he announced, and laughed. "Well, I guess you did see something. It must have been a cat that got in from outside. You must have scared it, and seen its eyes, and then it jumped past you to get away from all your screaming." He smiled. "Can't say I blame it. You yelled loudly enough to wake the dead."

Sharon felt a moment of doubt. Was that what had happened? Then she shook her head. "I closed the window last night," she replied. "And the eyes I saw were red. Aren't cats' eyes green or yellow?" She forced herself to look at the window and saw the deep scratches in the woodwork. The dirt on the floor was gray and sterile, like the dirt in the nightmare woods, not the backyard. If a cat had brought that here, and made those scratches, it was some unearthly cat indeed.

"Try and get back to sleep," her mother suggested. And, almost too casually, "I think I'd better make an appointment for you with that therapist. Don't you?"

Sharon looked at her parents and saw that they were worried about her, but they clearly didn't believe she had really seen anything. She started to say something, then stopped. What was the use? They'd never listen to her. "Whatever you say," she agreed dully.

"It's the best thing," her father told her. "She'll help you sort out what's going on and stop these terrible dreams you've been having." He closed the window firmly. "Good night."

Sharon clambered back into bed nervously, and her parents turned off the light. She could hear their footsteps and the quiet muttering of their voices as they returned to their own room.

A therapist! They thought she was imagining it all. Well, she wished that she was. That way, at least there was a hope she could unimagine it all and things would be back to normal again.

But she knew, deep inside herself, that it wasn't quite so simple.

Why were things so complicated? Just when everything seemed to be so perfect, she was plunged savagely back into the ongoing nightmare. Would there never be any peace for her?

Or would it be the long, cold peace of the grave?

NINE

Sunday passed slowly. Chiku called her after breakfast, demanding all the details of the previous night's date. Shaken by her dream, Sharon had to take a moment to gather her thoughts and realize that it had only been twelve hours since the dreamy date with Travis.

"Tell me all the gruesome details," Chiku gloated. "I want to know everything."

"He was a perfect gentleman," Sharon answered.

"Bummer. Oh well, maybe he'll misbehave next time."

Sharon giggled. It was difficult to stay in a grim mood with Chiku around. "I like him. It was a great date."

"Sounds historic to me. So, when's he taking you out again? Or has he had enough of you and wants a real girl? You can tell him I'm available."

"If he even looks at you, I'll kill you," Sharon promised. "Keep your grubby little hands off him."

"Ah-ha!" Chiku laughed triumphantly. "You've got it bad, girl. Sad, sad. So, when are you seeing him again?"

"I don't know. He didn't say. Maybe if you get off the phone he'll call me. Or . . . should I call him?" Sharon suddenly realized she didn't have his number, even.

"Whoa, don't you dare, girl," Chiku warned. "Let the guy do the chasing. It's beneath your dignity to bum calls from him. Make him do the work."

"That sounds pretty sexist. Is it more of the famous Williams advice?"

"Have you ever known it to fail?"

"I'm the one who had a date last night, not you," Sharon pointed out. "I'll listen to your advice when there's proof to back it up."

"Skeptic," scoffed Chiku.

They said good-bye and hung up, leaving Sharon in an agitated state of mind. Would Travis call her? Would he wait until he saw her at school? She eyed the phone, praying for it to ring. Naturally, it was silent. Gnawing at her lip, she pondered calling Travis. Would that be a good idea?

The morning passed slowly, burning at her nerves. Would he call? Should she call? Would anything happen?

Naturally, the phone rang just when she was sitting down to dinner. Sharon shot out from the dining room, then hesitated over it. Should she pick it up before the second ring? Would she look too eager? And—what if it wasn't Travis?

Decisions . . . She picked it up. "Hello?"

"Sharon." It *was* him! "Hi. I just called to see if you had a good time last night."

"Mmm? Oh, yeah. It was really great." *Oh, that was clever.* "Did you enjoy it?" *Oh, brother! This was pathetic! So boring.*

"With you? How could I not have fun?" he said in a low voice that sent shivers down her spine. "Listen, I've got to go—chores and stuff, you know? But I had to talk to you. See you tomorrow?"

"Yeah. See you then. Thanks for calling. 'Bye." Sharon put the phone down and stared at it. He had called. He had a good time. She felt like hugging herself.

"You want this dinner?" her father yelled from the other room. "Or should I have seconds?"

Sharon shot back in, unable to keep the smile off her face. Her mother nodded and said to her husband: "Told you. It was Mr. Wonderful. She's smiling again."

Mr. Anders winked. "Well, he'll have a good effect on our grocery bills too if this is how she eats after talking to him."

Sharon took the hint and resumed eating. But her thoughts weren't on food.

That night was quiet. No dreams, at least not that she could recall. And then it was Monday, and school. And Travis . . .

As Sharon padded to the bathroom for her shower, she could hear her mother downstairs making breakfast. Her father was rummaging around in the den, looking for some papers he'd brought home to work on. Whatever case he was on at the moment, he was certainly putting in plenty of extra work. She felt sorry for him, but not too much—he really enjoyed his job.

She never really thought about it much, but she did have a pair of terrific parents. Lots of the kids in her classes were from single-parent homes or crummy families. And there had been Jessica Turley, whose father had been abusing her. It got dragged through the local papers for weeks before he was jailed. She was still in and out of therapy. Sharon realized she was so lucky to have two parents that loved her and each other so much.

She turned on the water, adjusting the controls until it was just right, then stepped in. The heat and spray hammering against her body felt refreshing. She pushed her face under the flow, enjoying the massaging feel against her skin. Then she turned to reach for the soap, and opened her eyes.

The water was bright red.

The redness showered down around her, wet and heavy. Her mouth and nose caught the scent, the gagging bitterness of blood.

Sharon screamed, and the blood splattered into her open mouth, choking her. Throwing up her arms, she hunkered down in the stall, screaming again and again. The nauseating flow beat against her.

And then stopped. The shower door was wrenched open, and her mother gasped. Then she grabbed a towel and wrapped it about Sharon, dragging her out of the stall. Sharon grabbed at her mother, hugging her close and tight, gagging and choking. She felt her robe being wrapped around her, and then her father appeared in the doorway.

"What the—" he began, standing there, struck suddenly dumb.

Sharon turned to look at him, wiping redness away from her eyes and nose, unable to reply. She followed his gaze toward the shower. In a pool in the bottom, red liquid glistened.

Mr. Anders strode over and knelt down. Dipping a finger in the liquid, he sniffed it. "Paint!" he exclaimed, astonished.

"Paint?" Sharon echoed. She rubbed at a spot on her shoulder and smelled it.

It *was* paint, not blood. But she had been certain that before her parents had arrived the stuff had been hot, sticky blood. She had smelled it, felt it.

"How in blazes could that have happened?" her father mused. Then, leaving the room, he called back: "Hang on." Sharon heard him pull down the attic door and ladder, and then climb up.

"Goodness, you're a mess," her mother fussed. "This towel is going to be ruined. I'll never get the paint out of it."

Her father suddenly reappeared carrying a battered can with the lid half off. "I don't know," he muttered. "Maybe that cat got into the attic and knocked the can over. It's the one I used to redo the garage door last summer. Most of it's gone now." He nodded at the shower. "It must have come down through the roof somehow."

"It didn't come through the ceiling," Sharon said

in a low voice. "It came out of the shower itself. And it wasn't paint, it was blood."

Her father looked at her doubtfully, and she could see that he was worried as well as puzzled. And that he didn't believe her. Furiously, she pointed at the stall.

"Look!" she yelled. "If it came through the ceiling, wouldn't there be a stain there?"

"Calm down, honey," her mother said softly. But she and her husband both gazed at the ceiling of the stall.

There was no sign of paint there at all.

"Very peculiar," was all Mr. Anders could think of to say.

Sharon was shaking badly, but she managed to make her way to the downstairs bathroom. This one had a tub, and her mother had offered to stay with her while she washed the paint off. Sharon didn't care what her mother thought, and scrubbed furiously at her skin.

"That paint's ruined your hair, Sharon," her mother said, sighing. "You're going to have to have it cut short and let it grow out again."

"I just hope it *has* a chance to grow out again," Sharon muttered. Maybe she wouldn't live that long. . . . She caught the funny look her mother gave her and returned to scrubbing. Finally she felt clean again, and let her mother return to the kitchen while she toweled herself dry. Then she almost ran up the stairs to her room to get dressed.

Sharon caught sight of her hair in the mirror as

she did so. She'd always been so proud of her long, blond hair, hanging halfway down her back. Now it was flecked with red paint that stubbornly refused to come out. This, more than any horrors she had experienced so far, hurt the most. This *thing* attacking her had made a very bad mistake. She was no longer simply terrified. She was also furious.

She had no idea what was going on, or who was doing this to her, or why. But she was grimly certain of one thing: She wasn't going to give in. Not now, not ever. Whoever or whatever was behind this attack on her sanity might kill her, but it wouldn't ever defeat her. Staring into the mirror at her ruined hair, she promised: "I'll get you for this. I will."

"What's this?" Chiku grinned. "A new look? A strawberry blond with *real* strawberries?"

"Don't even try to joke about it," Sharon said darkly. "This was its latest attack on me." She told her friend about the new dream and the blood in the shower. The other kids were drifting past, laughing, talking, and waving at one another as they headed for classes. It all seemed so normal, so everyday. Like nothing so bizarre could ever have happened.

Chiku was at a loss to find anything to say for once, and Sharon smiled at her without any humor. "What's up? Aren't you going to call this another coincidence?"

The black girl shook her head. "No way. This is getting too freaking weird." She hesitated. "I did some more reading last night. And . . ." She seemed unsettled, then plunged on: "I think maybe you're being targeted by a supernatural entity."

"I'm *what?*"

"I think that something is trying to get at you." Chiku looked embarrassed, and even jumpy. "The more I've been thinking about things, the more I'm certain that you're not imagining it. I did some research into hauntings. I had kind of figured that you just had common or garden ghosts. But it turns out that there's a sort of whole chain of beings that people believe live in a sort of separate dimension. Somehow, one is breaking into *our* dimension." She held up her hand. "Mind you, I'm not saying that I believe all of this. But you're my friend, Sharon, and I believe *you.*"

Sharon was touched, and hugged the other girl. "Knock it off!" Chiku protested. "People will get the wrong idea about us."

When she was free, she continued to explain. "There's all kinds of creatures that a lot of people claim to have met at night, mostly. There's the kind that are like juvenile delinquents—they play jokes and tricks, just to annoy people. You know, like the leprechauns of Ireland."

"Whatever is after me isn't playing tricks," Sharon said.

"No. It is not a pixie. That leaves us with the powers, I guess."

"The powers?"

Chiku looked thoughtful. "You know—devils, fallen angels, demons, that sort of thing. Powers of

78

evil, creatures that delight in destruction. Things that like wrecking anything good."

Sharon shivered. "That sounds pretty close to the thing in my nightmare. It seems to enjoy watching this man kill me. Like it enjoys the killing. But there's more." Sharon struggled to put her feelings and fears into words. "It's like my dying is just the beginning of what it's after."

"Maybe it is," Chiku replied. "According to the legends, these creatures of the night get into inflicting suffering on people. But they really want the actual souls of people. So far, it sounds like this whatever-it-is has been tormenting you for fun. But if it's real, and it's one of these powers of evil, then it's going to get worse."

Sharon looked at her friend bleakly. "Gee, thanks. I feel better now."

"Come on, Sharon," Chiku answered. "If we can find out what this thing is, and why it's picking on you like this, then maybe we can figure out some way to get rid of it."

For the first time, Sharon felt a faint stirring of hope. "Get rid of it? Can we do that?"

Chiku shrugged. "It's all a matter of control," she explained. "According to Dad's books, you can control a power and force it to leave you alone. I'm just not sure how yet. I have to do some more reading up. But one thing I do know. These powers don't just pick people at random. They have to have a link of some sort with them. Otherwise we'd all be overrun with the icky little beasties. There has to be something that connects you to this monster in the woods."

"Like what?"

"I haven't gotten that far yet. But there must be a reason why it's after you, and not me, for example. We have to find out what the link is."

Sharon nodded. What Chiku was saying was something she'd have laughed at just a month ago. Now, however, it might be her only chance of ever living a normal life again. She was certain that Chiku was on the right track. The thing in her nightmare had claimed she belonged to it. Like it had a right to her, or something. But why? And—

A hand dropped onto her shoulder. Startled, Sharon yelled and jumped, hitting out with her books.

With a suppressed yelp, Larry toppled backwards, his own books scattering. Sitting up, he scowled. "Boy, you're sure jumpy in the morning, aren't you? What's up—miss your caffeine fix?"

Sharon gave him a poisonous look. "Don't ever sneak up on me like that again!"

Gathering his books, Larry nodded. "You betcha! Once is enough for me to take a hint." He switched moods, grinning at Chiku, who was stifling her laughter. "So, beautiful, how about coming over? I've got this great new video, called—"

"I don't want to know!" Chiku broke in. "It's undoubtedly something sick, perverted, and filled with disassembled bodies. I thought you said you could take a hint? The answer is no, *capiche?*"

For the first time, Larry seemed taken aback. He

looked from one girl to the other. "Boy," he finally said. "You two both got out of the wrong side of bed this morning."

Travis had joined them, without Larry's spotting his approach. He tapped Larry on the shoulder, almost causing him to collapse a second time. "Maybe," Travis suggested, "you're going about this whole thing the wrong way."

"What makes you the expert?" demanded Larry belligerently.

"The fact that I've got a date for the Halloween Dance on Friday." Travis smiled. Then he bowed slightly in Sharon's direction. "If you agree, that is."

Sharon smiled. Travis could brighten her mood without even trying. And if he had noticed the disaster that had happened to her hair, he didn't mention it. She'd have been mortified if he had. How could she tell him that she was haunted? "I'd love to."

"See?" He smiled at Larry. "Why don't you try it?"

Larry looked at Chiku, who had her head cocked to one side, studying him. For the first time in Sharon's memory, he actually looked uncertain of himself, and almost vulnerable. "Ah, well," he said, coughing. "Maybe later, okay?" He rushed off.

Chiku stared after him in amazement, then turned back to Travis. "Well, I don't know what you did, but you scared him right off."

The lazy grin didn't leave Travis's face. "He'll be back," he promised. "And I'll bet he asks you to the dance."

"What if you're wrong?" demanded Chiku. "Then what?"

He shrugged. "I'll break both his legs."

Slyly, Chiku suggested: "You could always take me to the dance, too."

Sharon gave a mock frown at this. "You'd better be right about Larry coming back," she warned Travis. "I'm not sharing you with anyone. Not even my best friend."

"Cheapskate." Chiku laughed, and ducked the slow punch Sharon aimed for her.

Sharon's mood had improved dramatically, and the thoughts of fallen angels, hauntings, and slashers were pushed back deep into her mind. She had a date for the dance!

TEN

Her mother met her after school and took her to get her hair cut. Sharon almost cried when the hairstylist there shook her head and pronounced the verdict that most of Sharon's long hair would have to go. She winced with each snip of the scissors, and couldn't say anything when she finally emerged at the end of her ordeal with a simple page-boy cut.

"It'll grow back," the girl said. Biting back a venomous retort with difficulty, Sharon just nodded and paid. As she was leaving, she looked back to see the girl pop a stick of gum in her mouth and start to sweep up the red-flecked locks. Fighting back tears, Sharon followed her mother to the car.

Things didn't improve at the next stop. This was a small professional building tucked away in a medical park. The receptionist nodded when Mrs. Anders gave their names, and buzzed through to tell Dr. Jablonski that they had arrived.

A moment later, Dr. Jablonski emerged from the

83

inner office. Sharon was surprised. She had expected the therapist to look like Dr. Ruth. Instead, she was a slim, brown-haired woman in her mid-thirties. She looked both pleasant and attractive, and shook Mrs. Anders's hand. She gestured toward one of the chairs and the inevitable pile of dog-eared magazines.

"Perhaps you'd be good enough to wait out here," she said.

"Well, I had thought . . ." Mrs. Anders began.

The therapist shook her head. "No, it's okay. I'll talk with Sharon alone. You can come in at the end, and I'll discuss things then."

Looking anything but certain, Mrs. Anders said: "Well, all right, I suppose."

"Good." The doctor gestured for Sharon to go ahead, then followed her into the inner office and closed the door.

Again, Sharon was surprised. The room was small but cozy. There was a desk and two comfortable-looking chairs. Several plants and abstract prints were all the decoration that the room possessed. She raised an eyebrow. "What, no couch?"

"Why? Are you tired?" Dr. Jablonski smiled, to show that she was joking. "No, no couch. The people who come to see me aren't crazy," the doctor said. "They merely have some unresolved emotional problems. I try and help them to see the root cause of their trouble, and equip them to deal with it."

"Really?"

"Really." Dr. Jablonski smiled. "If you won't take

it the wrong way, I'd be very happy if this were the only time I ever see you professionally."

"Well, that's one thing we can agree on."

"You sound angry."

Sharon looked at her. She'd reached her limit on being abused for one day. First the shower, then the loss of her hair, and now a therapist. She was over-reacting, she knew, but she couldn't help it. "I guess I am," she said.

"It's not uncommon. Many people would rather verbally attack me than attack their own problems."

Laughing, Sharon shook her head. "Believe me, I'd love to attack my problems. The trouble is that *they* attack me."

The doctor raised an eyebrow. "Want to tell me about it?"

Sharon hesitated, then shrugged. "Sure. What the heck. You're probably charging my folks a bundle for this, so they might as well get their money's worth." She paused. "I'm being hunted by a de-mon."

The doctor made an "I'm listening" face, so Sharon plunged on and told her about the dreams.

In the waiting room, Mrs. Anders nervously flicked through a magazine. She had no idea what it was, or what she was reading. She looked at the door to the inner office yet again, then caught the recep-tionist's gaze. The woman smiled, unemotionally, a professional reassurance that didn't work. Mrs. An-ders sighed.

Sharon was a terrific daughter, and she'd never

been more than the slightest problem. She and Henry were very proud of her, and always had been. Now, though, just being here seemed to imply that they had failed somehow—even after all their precautions. Sharon was suffering from something they couldn't help her with, or had maybe somehow caused. Had Henry been too absorbed with his caseload recently? Had she failed to be there when Sharon needed help?

What bothered her the most was that she couldn't prevent these terrible nightmares. And she had no other way to deal with the matter than by bringing Sharon to see this therapist. But it was going to be so painful to rake open all the old wounds. With a sigh, she returned to flicking through the magazines.

"So," the therapist mused, "you're having problems sleeping because of this dream."

"Wouldn't you?" challenged Sharon. "But it's not just the dream. Really weird things have been happening to me." She explained about the closet, the stolen knife, and the paint incident. Finally, she sat back and studied the doctor. After a long pause, Dr. Jablonski asked Sharon: "So you think that this . . . power of evil is out to get you?"

Sharon shrugged. "It's a theory that fits the facts the best. A lot better than coincidence, that's for sure."

"I don't like the word *coincidence*," Dr. Jablonski replied. "I prefer the word *pattern*. The human mind is very fond of finding patterns in everything. Haven't you ever stared at a carpet or abstract wallpaper some time and seen faces or shapes there? They aren't really in the paper or the rug, but your mind finds them anyway, because it wants to make order out of chaos. That's how the mind works. I think that's what's been happening in your case.

"You dream all the time, Sharon, but you forget most of them on waking. They're not important, or funny, or interesting enough. But sometimes something happens that's similar to an event in a dream. Then you feel that the dream predicted the event."

Sharon couldn't stop herself from laughing. "In other words, I'm imagining things, and the paint, the closet, and the knife are just wild coincidences that just happen to have matched my dreams?" She snorted in disbelief. "These dreams aren't just horrible thoughts I'm making up. They're very real."

"Of course they're real—to you." The therapist sat forward confidentially. "But that doesn't mean that they are objectively real. They couldn't be experienced by someone else, for example."

Sharon glared at her and grabbed a chunk of her short blond hair. "The paint in my hair was real enough. I had to have it butchered after school. The knife was stolen. The closet door was broken. How much more has to be real?"

Dr. Jablonski thought for a moment. "Do you have a boyfriend?"

Caught off guard by the question, Sharon frowned, then nodded.

"Is he a new boyfriend?"

"About a week or so. I only just met him. Why? What does this have to do with the dreams?"

"Everything." The doctor leaned forward in her chair again. "Sometimes a new relationship can produce a great deal of tension. In your subconscious, you may have some unresolved fears about it. You know: *Maybe I'm not good enough for him. Maybe I'll lose him. Maybe he's really a creep, and not the nice guy I think.* Or fears about facing your own sexuality. That kind of thing. Sometimes those fears are so buried we don't even know they're there. Then they surface in strange ways, like in our dreams."

"What?" Sharon laughed. "Right. I'm worried about this new guy, so I dream about being murdered?"

"Roughly that, yes."

Sharon shook her head. "That's the biggest load of . . . rubbish I've ever heard. In the first place, I just met Travis. In the second place, I was having these dreams before I even met him."

Dr. Jablonski sighed. "Look, Sharon, the human mind is a complicated machine. Sometimes it does very strange things. Don't you think you should examine all the possibilities?"

"I think you're the one who's hunting for a pattern here." Sharon was annoyed and didn't try to hide it. "I come in with a problem, and you start immediately thinking: *Ah, classic case seventeen: girl with hidden sexual fantasies.* Then you try and fit everything I say into that neat little theory, whether it works or not. And it doesn't." She glared at the therapist. "Do you believe in the existence of evil spirits, or forces?"

"Do you really feel that you need to invent some

mythic universe of dark forces to explain your problems away?" the doctor asked.

"See what I mean?" Sharon shook her head. "*You*
wrote off that whole possibility."

Dr. Jablonski paused and took a calming breath.
Then she faced Sharon again.

"Well, we still have to work out a resolution to
your sleeping problems. I think that what you need
to do is to confront your own feelings in this matter.
Face them head-on."

"I know what my feelings are," Sharon replied
heatedly. "Fear. And I meet them head-on. And get
killed for it."

Mrs. Anders jumped up and rushed over when
the door to the inner office opened. Dr. Jablonski led
a tense-looking Sharon out.

"Well, Doctor?" her mother asked, her nervous-
ness mixed with worry. "What do you think?"

"She thinks," Sharon said, "that I'm a sex bomb
looking for a place to explode." She raised her eyes
to the roof. "And I'll bet she wants me to sign up for
a whole course of treatment to defuse me."

"Sharon!" her mother exclaimed.

"Look, maybe I'd better wait in the car while you
talk to the shrink. This way I won't be tempted to be
rude again." Without waiting for an answer, Sharon
walked out. She heard her mother starting to apolo-
gize as the door closed behind her.

She didn't get into the car, but walked up and
down beside it, waiting. Was it possible that this
screwy doctor might be right? That it was just a case

of her mind freaking out for some reason? Maybe it was just something really simple and dumb like she had suggested.

No. It simply didn't add up. The dream felt real and completely out of her control. If this dream was really just a simple sex problem, surely she'd know? This dream felt too real, too terrifying. It was too clear, too detailed, too horrific to be something she was subconsciously inventing.

And no amount of mental gymnastics explained the rest of what was happening to her.

Her mother finally came out and gave her a funny look. "You were rude in there, Sharon," she said. "I'm surprised at you for acting like that."

"I know, and I'm sorry. But that woman just rubbed me the wrong way." Sharon felt her anger rising again and tried to keep it down. As they got into the car, she asked quietly: "Did she want me back again?"

"Yes." Mrs. Anders studied the road carefully before adding: "I think you should consider the possibility of going back to see her next week."

Sharon sighed and rolled her eyes. Trust the adults to stick together. And to completely dismiss whatever she might think about the whole problem. "Whatever you say," she agreed dully. She would face next week when it came.

ELEVEN

She was in the woods again. Blackness cloaked her and the chill wind pinched her skin. She realized that she wasn't alone. And, strangely enough, the panic hadn't begun to settle into her yet. Another change, after so long without change . . .

Sharon moved slowly forward and touched something in the darkness. A branch, but different.

There were leaves on it!

Suddenly, Sharon realized that not only the tree was alive. There was a carpet of grass under her bare feet. In the distance, she could hear the rustling of nighttime animals moving about.

The entire forest was alive!

A shaft of silver light penetrated the gloom. As she looked up, she could glimpse portions of the full moon through the foliage. The moon! Maybe that therapist had been right, after all, and somehow the dream was altered? It didn't seem at all hostile or frightening.

She pushed on, able to see her path for the first time. It was really very pretty here. Wherever she was, of course. There was a small clearing ahead, and someone there. Sharon stopped, suddenly fearful that it was the killer. Then she realized that the figure was a woman with auburn hair, dressed in a long, red nightgown. She was looking around in some surprise. Then she caught sight of Sharon and waved.

It was Dr. Jablonski!

Sharon rushed over to her, astonished to see her.

"Sharon?" the therapist exclaimed. "Why am I dreaming about you?"

"You're not dreaming about me." Sharon laughed. "This is *my* dream. I'm dreaming about you. This is the woods I told you about."

The doctor smiled. "But you said that it was dead and oppressive here. This is lovely."

"Well," Sharon conceded, "it isn't the same tonight as usual, but this is definitely the same woods. Just—well, different."

"I'll say." Dr. Jablonski looked around. "It's so peaceful here."

Sharon nodded. It was nothing like she had been expecting. "Maybe you were right, after all," she admitted. "Maybe it was all stress and worry inside of me creating the dream."

"No," said a low, familiar voice. "She was wrong. Dead wrong."

Suddenly chilled, Sharon spun around. It was the slasher, carrying the same dripping red knife. His hooded eyes gleamed, and his smile was as crooked as ever.

The doctor gave a sharp intake of breath. "Who . . . who are you?"

The man stepped forward. In the night sky, the full moon started to shift and change. In seconds, the silver glow was gone, bathed in deep redness. Then the moon cracked, like an egg, crumbling and spilling blood all over the forest. The liquid hissed as it touched the living things. Leaves, trees, grass, all smoldered, died, and crumbled. The icy wind carried away the ashes, leaving only the bare, dead soil once again. In the distance, Sharon could hear the abrupt screams of dying animals.

Sharon gasped as the falling spray left burning pain and raised ugly red welts on her skin. Dr. Jablonski bit back cries as drops sizzled onto her own skin.

Their tormentor laughed. "Recognize this place better now?"

Dr. Jablonski pushed past Sharon. "Who are you? What are you doing to us?"

He laughed again, a cold, dry laugh, as if he wasn't used to such a sound. "This is where I am, shrink. This is my land."

"No," Sharon said, with sudden conviction. "This is your prison."

The man turned his burning eyes on her. She could see depths of pain and hatred there. For her, or for someone or something else? "Bright kid, eh? Just like your mother." He smiled again, looking at the therapist. "Come on, Doc—I'm just a figment of her repressed urges, remember? What are you so scared of?"

Sharon realized that the doctor was trembling. She tried to touch her, to comfort her, but she was shaken free. She could barely see in the darkness, but she somehow knew that Dr. Jablonski was screwing up all of her courage. "That's all you are. I'll prove it." She stepped forward.

Fear overwhelmed Sharon. "No!" she screamed, darting after her. "Don't do it!"

But she was too slow. With a sneer, the man lashed out, sinking the knife deep into the doctor's chest. The woman barely had time to look stunned, then she reached down, with a low, rattling cry. The red nightgown became a darker, wetter shade. The man wrenched his hand free, and Dr. Jablonski started to fall.

In her face was fear, bewilderment, and terrible pain. Trying to stop the bubbling fountain of blood in her breast, she whispered: "Run . . ." Then she fell to the ground, unmoving.

Shaking, Sharon looked up at her tormentor. His grin was back, and he waved the dripping knife in her face. She could smell the thick tang of fresh blood. "Now you know it isn't paint, don't ya?" he sneered.

Blind panic set in. With a cry, Sharon whirled and ran. Anywhere, it didn't matter where, just away from the body and the man with the knife. She ran, heedless of the brambles that scratched at her, the branches she stumbled into. Scuttling, chittering things ran alongside her, and from time to time she felt little sharp fangs nipping at her flesh. But she could see nothing of what the things might be. Striking out wildly at them, she heard them dance away, only to close in again when she staggered onward.

They were driving her, she realized! Making her turn and run where they wanted! She attempted desperately to break free and get through them. But some creature fell on her from the trees. It stank of soil and decay, and thin, hairy legs clawed over her shoulder. She could feel it making for her face. She slapped at it and felt tiny teeth bite, but she knocked it free and ran.

In the direction they wanted.

Finally, as always, she could take no more. Every panting breath burned her throat and chest. Every time her feet hit the ground, the jarring in her legs was worse. Each branch seemed stronger, sharper, and more painful as she hit it. Eventually, she dropped to the forest floor, heaving and crying with fear.

One of the insect-things poked at her, and her skin crawled at the touch of tiny feelers. But she didn't have the strength to draw away. She waited for them to attack her, for the tiny teeth to tear at her flesh. Instead, still chittering softly, the things faded back into the shadowy woods.

She rolled onto her back, seeing nothing but red blotches in her eyes as the blood pounded through her. Drawing in deep, long breaths, she tried to calm her shattered nerves.

She realized that he was there, watching her, enjoying her panic, feasting on her pain. She managed to get her elbow under her and levered herself un-steadily into a sitting position. He smiled at her, but there was only hatred and fear in his blazing eyes.

"You can't get away," he told her. "You never could. You never had a chance."

Sharon tried to fight down the bile that rose in her throat, and shook her head. He wanted her to be terrified. That was the whole point of this chase. Not just to kill her, but to scare her to the edge as well. She tried to summon up all of her resolve, all of her strength.

"I can get away," she told him. "There is a chance. There must be."

He laughed icily. "Not for you," he said. "You belong to him. You always have."

Sharon could feel the other here now. The un-man, the power of darkness. It was in the ring of trees, watching, brooding, waiting. It was feeding on her fear, she knew. Like a meal—her terror was the spice that gave her taste to the thing. It had to have her not merely afraid, but utterly paralyzed with fright.

She wouldn't do it! She wouldn't! "I'll fight you," she promised hoarsely. "And I'll win."

"You?" The voice was the thin, dry rustle of death. In the one word was packed contempt, and hunger, and desire.

And, just maybe, a little fear. Or was she simply allowing her hopes to get the better of her?

"I can kill you any time," the man said, stepping forward, showing her the dripping knife. "You can't stop me. How can you hope to fight *him?*" He nodded backward toward the trees.

Sharon couldn't take her eyes off the tip of the knife as he lowered it toward her. She felt so defenseless in her nightgown. The knife came down to her throat and rested there.

Suddenly, everything welled up within her: her fears, the panic, the fatigue, all of it was lost in a surge of uncontrollable anger. How dare this crazy man try and kill her, over and over? He'd already killed Dr. Jablonski, at least in this dream. Okay, the therapist had been a bit of a jerk, but she had tried to help in her own way. All Sharon could think of was that she wanted to hurt this man who was sadistically playing games with her.

Her fingers closed about a handful of the dead soil. With an animal scream of hatred, she threw it directly into his eyes. He reeled back, wiping at his face and cursing, the knife no longer at her throat. She jumped forward, knocking his hand aside, and started punching him wildly anywhere she could reach. She gave him a good crack in his left eye before he managed to push her away from him.

He seemed completely surprised by her unexpected and furious attack, giving ground before her. Sharon yelled at him, using language her parents would have been shocked at, hitting him back for all of the anguish he had ever caused her, determined that this time she would not die. This time—

Something cold and hard as steel gripped her body. She could see nothing, but felt a huge hand clasped around her, squeezing the breath and life out of her. She gasped, unable to inhale, and stopped fighting. The gigantic hand pressed harder, and she heard the blood singing in her ears and saw nothing but vivid yellow flashes. Giddily, she felt her body being lifted from the ground, and felt the warm, fetid breath of the creature that had snatched her up. The power of evil . . .

With a scream of fury, the man leaped back at her, the knife in his hand flashing downward. There was a moment of sharp, intense agony—

—and she awoke, thrashing in her bed. With a deep, satisfying breath that filled her lungs again, she stopped struggling and lay still. It was over for the night. And she had *almost* won! She had fought back and nearly beaten the man-monster. It was only the un-man that had taken her by surprise, other-wise . . .

She stiffened in panic. She had heard . . . there it was again! Breathing.

There was something in her room.

She opened her eyes and stared into the gloom.

The breathing sound increased.

She sat up suddenly and looked around. There, in the shadows by the open closet door, she could make out something. It was vaguely the shape of a man, but much taller. It had to stoop beneath the ceiling. Twin eyes of fire stared back at her.

There was another sound, the beating of wings, and something dropped from above directly onto her face. She barely had the chance to scream before it hit her, enveloping her face, and clung to her skin.

She could smell mustiness about it, gagging and choking her.

In terror, she tore at it, clawing it free. The lights snapped on, and her parents were there in the doorway.

Otherwise the room was empty.

She had the thing that had fastened onto her face in her right hand, and it was unmoving now. She glanced down at it, expecting to see some animal. Instead, it looked like a newspaper clipping. Startled, she lifted it up to look at it closer.

It was dated November 1, 1974, and was yellowed and dry with age. Puzzled, she began to read. Sharon caught a glimpse of the headline: PENNSYLVANIA SLAYING. Then her attention was gripped by the accompanying photo.

It was her. It was her face in the picture.

Then the paper was snatched from her hand and she looked up to see her mother, pale and trembling. "Where did you get this?" she demanded.

"I don't know," Sharon answered, surprised by the force of the question. "It just hit me, and I pulled it off my face. What is it?"

"Nothing," her father said, curtly, with an uncharacteristically grim face. "Come on, Deb. We'd better get back to bed." He looked at Sharon, annoyed. "And so had you, young lady. You've woken us up enough these past few nights. Go to sleep."

"But, Dad, what is that—"

"*Go to sleep!*" he thundered and turned his back on her.

Puzzled, angered, and hurt by his tone, Sharon

could do nothing but lie back. As he and her mother left the room, the light was clicked off. Sharon heard her mother say something, and then her father angrily cut her off. The other bedroom door slammed.

What was all of that about? Her father's weird behavior disturbed her the most. He hadn't been so cold the last few times she'd woken them up, and she couldn't see why he should start now. What could make him so nervous about an old news clipping?

It obviously meant something to both her parents —but what? And why did it have her picture on it? And that date—November 1, 1974. She would have barely been a few days old then. She'd been born on October 30th of that year. So the picture couldn't be of her. It must be of someone who looked just like her.

The headlines had been about a murder . . .

There was a link there, she knew. That creature from her dream had left her the clipping. She was certain of this. It had wanted her to see it for some reason—just as surely as her parents didn't want her to see it. Troubled, unable to resolve her many questions, she tossed and turned. Uneasily, she finally managed to drift off to sleep again.

TWELVE

Breakfast the following morning was very subdued. Neither of her parents would meet Sharon's looks, nor did they seem willing to talk, not even to each other. In moody, tense silence, the meal was an ordeal that Sharon was glad to end.

At school, she barely saw or heard the other students about her. She caught a few comments about her new hairstyle, which didn't improve her mood. She *hated* her hair short. She was lost in anger and puzzlement, and it wasn't until Chiku jogged her elbow that Sharon suddenly realized that her friend had been talking to her for two or three minutes. "Sorry," she mumbled.

"It's okay," Chiku answered. "One thing about talking to yourself is that at least you can be sure of an intelligent audience. Anyhow, I asked you how you're doing. You look like you lost a fight with a nightmare again."

"I guess I did." Sharon related the details of the

101

previous night's dream, concluding: "Both Mom and Dad are acting like clams today. They won't even talk about that clipping. But it must be important somehow."

Chiku frowned. "Boy, your life gets weirder every day. Okay, let's think for a moment. If that clipping is important, surely it's the power of evil that thinks so. Maybe you'd be better off not reading it?"

"I don't know," Sharon admitted miserably. "But —that picture in the story. It looked exactly like me. Yet this girl died at about the same time I was born. I've got to know more, Chiku, whatever the cost. I can't get it out of my mind."

"No problem, then." Chiku patted her on the back. "Your friend Madame Williams sees all, knows all, and blabs all. All we have to do is take a trip to the library in town after school. They've got one of these machines that has newspapers on microfilm going back to the turn of the century. You know the date you're looking for, and that the murder was in Pennsylvania. Should be a cinch to find."

"Right!" Sharon had completely forgotten about that possibility. "Then maybe we'll know something more about what's happening."

"You know," Chiku said thoughtfully, "there is one possibility, if you go for all this Shirley MacLaine stuff about reincarnation. What if you're that girl who was murdered, and you're somehow reliving her final hours?"

Sharon considered this. It did make a loopy kind of sense that she'd have dismissed a few days ago. Finally, though, she shook her head. "No, the man and the *thing* both call me by name in the dream. Unless her name was Sharon, too, I can't go for this reincarnation thing."

"At least you managed to fight back last night," Chiku added. "Girl, I'm proud of you."

"It didn't do me much good."

"It's not the result that counts here," said Chiku. "It's the fact that you suppressed your terror enough to even try it. Maybe you'll win out soon on this." She stopped, looked, and did a double take. "*Larry?*" she exclaimed. "What on earth are you up to?"

Sharon spun around to see a strangely subdued Larry trying to slide past them without being seen. He was so furtive-looking, she was completely confounded. Normally, he was the brightest, breeziest, most self-confident boy she'd ever seen. And he never missed a chance to try and chat up Chiku.

He was wearing sunglasses.

"Er, hi," he said, waving his hand slightly and inching away. "I gotta go."

"Shades?" Chiku laughed. "Larry, you're all confused. This is October, not August. You don't need shades." She reached out to take them from him, but he batted her hand down.

"Hey, leave me alone," he snapped.

Chiku was obviously as puzzled by this behavior as Sharon was. "What's with you?" she asked, hurt. Then, while he was groping for an excuse, she grabbed the shades.

His left eye was swollen and mottled with purple bruises.

He snatched back the sunglasses and stuck them

back on. "I . . . walked into a door in the dark," he muttered feebly. Then he turned and ran.

Chiku stared after him. "I swear, I don't know why I like him." She sighed. "He's almost as weird as you." Then she saw the shocked expression on Sharon's face. "What's up? Never seen the results of a lost fight before?"

Shaking her head, Sharon fought back the fear she was experiencing. "It's not that," she managed to say. "But last night, I threw dirt into the maniac's eyes, and then punched him. I'm sure I got in a hefty blow to his *left* eye. . . ."

"And you think that because Larry's got a black eye . . ." Chiku's voice trailed off. "Sharon—Larry may be a bit of a space cadet at times, but I can't believe he'd ever try to hurt someone."

"No?" countered Sharon. "He's the one who loves horror flicks, remember? Are you sure he'd never try to duplicate one of them in real life?"

Chiku looked at her friend uncertainly. Finally, she managed to say: "It just doesn't sound like Larry to me."

"Well, maybe there's a side to Larry we're only just beginning to see." Sharon remembered the story she'd heard from Jenn, but bit back the urge to tell Chiku. It wouldn't help. "Don't forget he seemed awfully keen to avoid us this morning—which isn't like him at all."

"Come on," Chiku said. "Give him a break. He lost a fight and was embarrassed. That's all. Guys hate to be seen as losers. Ruins their macho self-images and all that junk."

Sharon shrugged. "You believe what you want. I'll keep my thoughts to myself until I get further proof."

"Proof of what?" Travis had walked up to them from behind. He smiled at Sharon and almost dispelled the dark mood that had settled on her. "You're not still doing your math homework, are you?"

"No." She smiled back. "Just personal stuff."

He nodded. "You look great with your hair like that. It suits your face. Sort of frames its beauty, you know. Like one of those old masters' oil paintings. Classic gorgeous."

His words sent chills through her. Some were of fear—his mention of oils, and paintings, and the pain of losing her hair. Some were of pleasure—*He thinks I'm gorgeous!* "So," she finally managed. "You want to take the new-look me out?"

"Can you wait till Thursday?"

Sharon had to laugh. "I'm not that desperate," she assured him. "I can wait. But not too long."

"Okay, I'm warned." He threw up his hands in surrender. "Incidentally, a little bird tells me that your birthday's coming up."

Sharon glared at Chiku. "I don't need two guesses who."

"Cheep, cheep," Chiku peeped, and ignored the filthy look Sharon shot her way.

"Well, I'm glad she told me. I'd hate to miss it. You having a party?"

Sharon snorted. "I'm too old for cake and clowns."

"Well, how about a movie?"

"It depends which one," she answered.

"Comedy, I promise." Travis grinned. "No violence. I scare easily."

Sharon nodded. "Sounds like fun. And I could do with some."

"Great. Thursday, then." He waved and set off for classes. Sharon stared after him, her suspicions and worries temporarily forgotten. Maybe it would be a pretty good day after all.

After school, Chiku and Sharon stopped off at the library downtown. Chiku led the way to the reference librarian. He was a cheery, middle-aged man, starting to bald. When Chiku explained that they were looking for a news item, he led them to one stack of reference books.

"Newspaper indexes," he explained. "They're produced each year for most papers. Just pick the year you need, then look up what you can in the index. That'll give you any reference dates. Once you have that, I'll show you what to do."

Chiku handed the 1974 volume for the local paper to Sharon, and took the identical volume for *The New York Times*. "Let's start hunting."

After a few tries, Sharon found what she was after in the *Philadelphia Inquirer* of October 1, 1974. The librarian checked his data-base files.

"Aren't computers great?" he asked. "All I have to do is to tell it the date and page and column numbers . . ." He tapped these in as he was speaking. "And then wait." After a very short while, a sheet of paper dropped into the printout tray. "And there we are."

It was a short article, with a picture—not the same clipping that had been in her room, but on the same story. And with the same photo of the murdered girl. It was a little grainy but bore an unmistakable, uncanny likeness to Sharon.

What was most disturbing was that the girl in the picture had her blond hair in a short, page-boy cut, just as Sharon now did . . . since yesterday.

She and Chiku took the piece to one of the tables and read it quickly through:

Paineston, Penn.—The body of a brutally murdered young woman was discovered early this morning by police in this small rural village. The victim, Shanna Bayer, 18, was a member of the Lost Arts Community, a commune of artists from New York City that relocated here less than six months ago. It was founded by noted pop artist Johnny Wilde.

Police Chief van Doren told this paper that his men are investigating the slaying, and that as yet there have been no arrests.

The victim was discovered due to the concern of relatives, who contacted the police and insisted on a search for her when she could not be found at the Lost Arts Community.

Chiku frowned when she had finished. "I don't get it," she admitted. "That girl looks just like you, but I can't see any connection."

"I can," Sharon said, a dull throbbing in her heart. "Mom's maiden name was Bayer."

"Oh." Chiku stared at the photo again. "Did she have a sister?"

"She's never talked about one. Or much about her family, for that matter." Sharon struggled through her memories. "She did tell me that her father died in 1970, and her mother a year or so later. And that she had no living relatives."

The black girl shrugged. "So, what do you think?"

Sharon stared at her friend, pain in her eyes. "I think it's time Mom and I had a talk."

Mrs. Anders looked up as Sharon walked slowly into the kitchen. "Finished your schoolwork already?" she asked. She was trying to sound casual, but Sharon could read the tension in her voice. Without replying, she handed over the newspaper page. Her mother barely glanced at it before sighing.

"I've been waiting for this," she admitted. "And dreading it." She dried off her hands. "I suppose it was wrong of Henry and me not to tell you before, but—well, we really didn't see any need."

"Tell me what?" Sharon demanded impatiently.

"Come on." Her mother led the way into the living room and sat on the sofa. "It's not easy to say, so I'd better be blunt, I guess. Sharon, your father and I—" She broke off and shook her head sadly. "I'd better stop saying that. Sharon, you're not actually our daughter. Your mother was my sister, Shanna." She gestured at the clipping. "This Shanna Bayer."

THIRTEEN

Sharon was stunned. She had been trying to imagine all kinds of reasons for her mother never having talked about her sister, but somehow this one had never occurred to her. She wasn't their child, but their niece! Adopted . . .

Her whole world seemed so fragile, as if one touch might send it all crashing about her ears. She shook her head dully, trying to reject the news, but it stuck in her mind with terrible clarity. It explained the resemblance between her and the dead girl, but very little else.

Mrs. Anders looked at her, obviously sympathetic to the emotions Sharon was going through. "I'm sorry we never told you before," she said softly. "But we did it to spare you knowing what happened to your mother."

"The murder."

"Well, that, yes. But there was a lot more the papers never got hold of, thankfully." She sighed, and paused, clearly gathering her thoughts and emotions.

"Tell me about it," Sharon demanded. She stared at her mother—no, her *aunt*! "I need to know everything."

Nodding, Mrs. Anders said slowly: "Well, that clipping last night was what started this. I don't know how it got to your room, but I knew when I saw it that we'd have to tell you the whole story. . . ." She steeled herself and began.

"My parents died when I was in my early twenties. It left just Shanna and myself. Shanna was seventeen, and looked terribly like you. But she was a wild spirit, and when our mother died, she got worse.

"She refused to stay with me and ran off to join this art group in New York, saying that society had failed her and our generation. They were all like that in the group. They were all pretty young, and filled with odd ideas. Well, I couldn't get Shanna to leave the group, and I knew that they weren't really very good for her. They were mostly into the peace thing, and Eastern religion, and drugs. Oh, pretty mild stuff, I guess, back then, and Shanna wasn't stupid enough to get into that side of it.

"There were about forty people in the community, and they all renounced marriage as shackles placed on people by society to legalize sex and keep them in line. Shanna fell for that idea. She refused to let society tell her what she could or couldn't do, she told me.

"Well, this Lost Arts place seemed to be producing very little art, and a lot of bad news. Their leader, a man called Johnny Wilde, decided that they'd be better off away from the corruption of society. They moved out to this old farm in Paineston, Pennsylvania. Back to the earth, they said. There they kept pretty much to themselves and went into their rejection of society wholeheartedly. They raised their own food, cut off the electricity, that kind of thing. I don't think they really thought out what they were doing too well. Apparently several of the girls became pregnant, including Shanna.

"She hadn't been in touch with us much. A letter now and then. In the meantime, I had met and married your fath—Henry. He was a struggling lawyer back in those days, but we were happy. The only thing was that we couldn't have children of our own. We decided that we'd work hard for a few years till Henry was established, then maybe adopt. Shanna didn't like Henry—called him a tool of repression. So we really didn't know much about what was happening to her. Then, out of the blue, we got a phone call from her.

"She'd gone to one of the neighboring farms, it seems, and used their phone. There weren't any at the commune. She didn't make much sense—just scared, rambling sentences. Henry calmed her down and got some of the story out of her. She'd just had her baby and was sick and weak, but she'd taken the child—you—and run. She kept saying that *he* was trying to kill her, or the child, but she was too ill to make much sense.

"Henry told her to stay where she was, and we'd

pick her up. The farmer gave us directions to his place. Then, as we set off, he called the police.

"When we got to the farm, Shanna was gone. The police were there, and the farmer. His wife had you safe and sound, but nobody knew what had happened to my sister. Henry took over and insisted that I look after you. He, the farmer, and the police then searched the area. Shanna had just run off into the night, we were told, but had deliberately left you behind. Well, after about an hour, they found her—dead." Mrs. Anders paused and bit her lip, her hands twisted tightly in her lap.

"How did she die?" Sharon broke in. She had to know.

"Stabbed to death," Mrs. Anders replied. She was clearly reliving that horrible night in her memory. Sharon reached out and took her hand. Her mother clutched at her, drawing on her unvoiced support. "Terribly stabbed, Henry told me. More than twenty times, all in the chest. There was blood all over.

"Anyway, the police set up a search, but they didn't find much. They were convinced that the killer was from the art commune—why else would Shanna have fled it? But nobody there would talk, and they couldn't pin the killing on anyone. Wilde especially was unhelpful, and the police were almost certain he was the killer. He was known to have a terrible temper, especially when anyone disagreed with him or disobeyed one of his rules. And we're pretty sure that he was the one who was your father. But we can't be certain.

"Well, the whole thing simply had to be filed away in the end, unsolved. Nobody liked that, but without witnesses or any real evidence, what else could be done?"

Sharon was reeling from all of this, but she managed to ask: "What about Wilde? Did he just get away with it?"

"No, not really. Henry and I took charge of you, and he was livid. He insisted that you were a member of his commune, born there and belonging there. Henry faced him down, telling him that there was no record of a father, and that I was your closest living relative by law. We intended to adopt you straight away, you see. Well, Wilde went—wild, I suppose. He tried to hit Henry, and the police took him away. He was given a short stay in jail for assault, and we managed to get the adoption pushed through. We thought that would settle it.

"Then, one night, we heard a noise from your room. This was in our old house, out near New York City, not here. We found Wilde had broken in and was trying to kidnap you. You must have been about three months old at the time. Henry attacked Wilde —a real tiger! You'd have been proud of him. I called the police. That time, Wilde was convicted of attempted kidnapping, burglary, the whole lot. He was given five years in jail for that.

"We were expecting trouble again, so we decided to move. We bought this house, didn't tell anyone where we were going, and left at night. Wilde never did find us again. Then we read a week or so after the move that he'd been killed, too, and that was that."

"He's dead?"

"Oh yes." Mrs. Anders thought back. "The neighbors in a run-down building that he had an apartment in called the police one night. They said there was some horrible fight going on in his room. When the police arrived, they found Wilde dead. Someone had stabbed him to death, just like your mother was killed. The police didn't find any clues, and nobody had been seen entering or leaving the room. He's another unsolved death. I hate to say it, but we were very glad when we heard about it. We'd been so worried about him trying to kidnap you again. He seemed obsessed about getting you back."

Sharon nodded. She was trying to sort out the whirling emotions within her head. She was just coming to grips with the facts, and they were beginning to make a stark, scary pattern at last.

Mrs. Anders, misinterpreting her daughter's silence, placed a hand on Sharon's arm. "I hope you don't think too badly of us for not telling you all of this before. But we were worried about hurting you if you learned the truth about your mother. It's not easy for a young woman to discover that she's illegitimate and adopted. I'm sorry."

Sharon was close to tears. "Don't be silly," she finally managed to say. "Maybe you and Dad aren't my biological parents, but you're still Mom and Dad, and always will be." She hugged her mother. "I love you both very much, and I know you really love me, too." She wiped her nose and dabbed at her eyes. "It's just these nightmares I've been having."

"Yes, I can imagine." Mrs. Anders looked relieved that she'd finally told the full story and cleared her conscience at last. "Henry thinks that perhaps they're caused by a sort of jumbled memory of those events. Me, I doubt you could remember any of that, even subconsciously."

"You said you'd kept clippings about the story," Sharon said slowly. "Can I look at them now?"

"I don't see why not. Hold on, I'll get the book." Mrs. Anders left the room.

Sharon tried to concentrate. The fact that she was adopted seemed somehow remote to her. She couldn't even begin to understand what her birth-mother must have been like to live in that terrible commune. But the fact that both her mother and her possible-father had been killed in the same way —slashed to death—and that the man in her night-mares was an artist and a slasher scared the heck out of her. Maybe there was something in the clippings that would help her understand what was going on.

"Here they are." Mrs. Anders reappeared with a scrapbook. "All kinds of things in there."

Nodding, Sharon opened it and started to look for something, anything, that might help to explain what was happening to her.

One clipping caught her eye, and she stopped dead, staring at it. She could feel herself going ice-cold, and the picture on the clipping burned into her mind.

Her mother peered over her shoulder. "Oh, yes," she said. "That's Johnny Wilde."

Numbly, Sharon nodded. She couldn't speak, just stared at the face. The very familiar face.

Her killer in the nightmares . . .

FOURTEEN

Later, Sharon curled up in the den on the phone with Chiku. With many interruptions, she finally managed to update her friend.

"Awesome," Chiku said, after a short silence. "Do you feel kind of funny, finding out you were adopted?"

Sharon tried to sort out her emotions on the issue. "Sort of," she finally agreed. "I mean, Mom and Dad are still the same people. But to know that my birth-mother was Mom's sister . . . I guess it's unsettling, more than anything. I'll adjust, I guess."

"Yeah. You're the kind that bounces back. But aren't you mad that they lied to you for so long? I would be." Chiku laughed. "I used to think I was adopted once, you know. My father always said he wished I was—adopted by somebody else. Then he'd get some peace."

Sharon giggled. "You drive him crazy, I'll bet." Then she thought about her own reactions. "No,

I'm not mad at them. They just did what they thought was best and sort of hoped I'd never find out about my real mother. Putting it off, I guess."

"Well," Chiku suggested, "maybe this will stop the nightmare?"

Sharon felt a sudden surge of hope. "What? How . . . how could it?"

"Well, you know now that Johnny Wilde killed your real mother. Maybe that's all the dream was about? You know, maybe your subconscious sort of added up tiny little hints that you didn't really notice over the years, and the dream was your subconscious trying to get the truth through to you?"

Sharon considered the idea. "No, I doubt it," she finally sighed. "I mean, the dream does have some bearing on the past, but it's *me* in the dream, and Wilde and the thing call me by name. And the clipping and Mr. Levine's art knife weren't things I could have dreamed up. I just wish I could figure out the connection, though, between what happened to Shanna Bayer and what's happening to me. I feel so helpless. I know how the dream will progress, and that I'll get killed in it."

"So, change the game. Don't let them set the rules. Start taking over, no matter how little."

"What do you mean?"

Chiku paused. "Well, for starters, you said you're always wearing in your dream what you wore to bed. Well, does that have to be a nightgown?"

An idea started to form in Sharon's mind. "No," she said, slowly. "No, it doesn't . . . Chiku, you're brilliant."

"I know," her friend replied modestly. "And destined for great things, too."

"I've taken enough abuse already," Sharon vowed. "The next time my dream comes back, I'm really going to let them have it."

"Go get 'em, tiger!"

Sharon hung up the phone, her hopes rekindled. She glanced up as her father entered the den, looking unsure of himself. He'd obviously arrived home while she was on the phone, and must have spoken to her mother.

"Hi, Sharon," he said nervously. "Deb tells me that you know about her sister now."

She nodded. "Mom told me all about it," she said, understanding his uncertainty. She rushed over and hugged him. "I'm glad I know the truth, but it really doesn't change much, does it?"

He hugged her back ferociously. "No, I'm glad it hasn't. We love you so much. We were just trying to save you the pain of the truth. I guess we should have known it couldn't be kept secret forever. But we just put off telling you."

Sharon nodded and freed herself from the hug. "I understand, Dad—honestly, I do. It must have been horrible for you, finding . . . Shanna like that."

She could see the grim memories in his eyes. "Yes," he said finally. "It was a horrible time for all of us. I'm just glad it's behind us now."

But it isn't, Sharon thought to herself. *Johnny Wilde hasn't given up just because he's dead. But maybe I can somehow end it at last. . . .*

* * *

That night, as Sharon lay in bed, she was certain that, this time, she would be able to make a difference. The only thing that really bothered her was how Larry might fit into it. Surely it couldn't be a coincidence that he was a slasher-movie freak, and that the day after she had smacked Johnny Wilde in the eye in her nightmare Larry had a black eye at school. But there was no way she could figure out how he fit into the pattern that was emerging.

She fell asleep grimly resolved on one point: This time, she wouldn't run. This time, she would face her fears—and her real father. . . .

She was standing in the dark, oppressive woods again, but this time the panic was conspicuously absent. The same chill wind blew, the same shadows crawled across the ground. But Sharon didn't care. She had won at least one minor point. She had worn her jeans, sweater, and sneakers to bed. And now, she was in the evil forest fully dressed.

Score one for her.

The wind clawed at her, as if furious for being locked out, and she smiled to herself. Chiku was right. Once you knew the rules, then maybe you could win the game.

Time to go for broke. "Come on out!" she yelled into the darkness. Her voice echoed around, bouncing from hollow, dried-out trees. "I know you're there! There's no point in hiding."

Something touched her shoulder and she spun around.

It was Johnny Wilde. Slightly stooped, he glared at

her from his hooded eyes. Was it her imagination, or did he look thinner, more haggard? Still, he held his murderous knife ready, the blood/paint dripping into the blackness.

For the first time ever, Sharon felt no fear. She was no longer uncertain and terrified by him.

"I know who you are," she told him contemptuously.

"Do you?" he asked. "Really?"

"Yes. You're a failed artist who stabbed my mother to death. And now you're after me. But you won't get me."

His eyes flickered backward, over his shoulder, for a moment. Then his lip curled in a sneer. "Haven't you forgotten something? I'm also your father."

"So you say." She refused to give ground to him. "But there's no proof. It could have been anyone."

"It was me." He sounded completely certain, and Sharon discovered that she believed him. It made no difference in her feelings for him.

"You make *me* sick," Sharon answered, wondering how far she could push him in her search for answers. "How could you kill my mother the way you did? Why do you want to kill me?"

Again, he glanced over his shoulder. There was no sign of the un-man. "I never wanted to kill her," he admitted. "That wasn't the plan. But she wouldn't do what I told her. And she *had* to. Otherwise . . . It was you I wanted all along. *You* were what I needed, not her." He stared intently at her, and despite her resolve, Sharon shuddered. "My firstborn." Then he grimaced. "But she took you

121

away, wouldn't let me have you. She ran. I went after her. She spat on me, clawed at my eyes. I had the knife, and I stabbed and stabbed and . . ." His voice faded away, and he just stood there for a moment, shaking slightly. The knife in his hand dripped softly. He looked up again. "And she was dead.

"That dumb lawyer and Shanna's sister had you. They wouldn't give you back to me. And the police took me. When I could, I tried to get you back again, but they . . . they interfered again. I couldn't help it." His voice died into the sighing of the wind.

"But why did you want me?" Sharon asked. "What did it mean to you? You didn't love me."

"Love?" He spat on the dead soil. "Love is for fools and cowards. No, *hate* is what matters. Hate and power. I didn't even hate you, though. You were my firstborn, and there's power in that. I had promised you to *him*."

Revelation hit her like a punch in the stomach. She stared at her father in disgust. "So that's it," she breathed. "The power of darkness. You promised the evil one the sacrifice of your firstborn, didn't you? In return for something."

"Yes," he agreed, staring at her almost hungrily. "He wanted you, a fresh soul to devour. But Shanna found out. She wanted to keep you. She was a fool! I told her—you were promised, and I had to sacrifice you. But she wouldn't listen. She never did." He licked his lips, slowly. "But you're here now, aren't you? And very, very close to death. Now I can fulfill my promise, can't I?"

"No." Sharon stared at him in contempt. "Your only power over me was ignorance. I was scared because I didn't understand. Well, now I understand—you're a pathetic, sadistic, stupid jerk, and I despise you!"

The glow in his eyes burned more brightly, and he raised the knife. "Say hello to death," he told her.

The look of utter contempt still on her face, Sharon shook her head. "No. I'm not going to die. You aren't going to win this time." She pulled her sweater up slightly, reaching for her father's large hunting knife, which she had strapped to her waist. It was here with her, in her dream, as she had prayed it would be. She drew it and held it ready. "You can try, but you won't win."

He stared at the knife she held in a mixture of astonishment and terror. "No!" he finally cried. "No! It isn't fair! It isn't fair! I should have won!" Abruptly he fell to his knees, throwing his arms over his face. "I can still win!"

"You could never win." It was the soft, sighing voice of the un-man. There was no visible sign of him, but Sharon could feel the chill of his approach despite her warm clothing. "You were a weak fool always, Wilde."

"No!" Johnny Wilde screamed. "Mercy!"

"Mercy?" The voice sounded almost amused. "Come now—you know that's one attribute I simply don't possess. Mercy indeed!"

Sharon could see nothing of the creature in the darkness, but there was a tingling fear all over her body. She knew it was coming closer, and she wanted to run. The terror she had vowed not to feel was growing within her, getting ready to burst and flood her with horror and panic.

Then Wilde screamed. His body was wrenched from the ground, as if by some unseen hand. His skin seemed to collapse inward, rotting on his bones. He screamed again, and Sharon heard a ripping sound, like a giant's claw tearing into his flesh. There was a brief silence, then Wilde's body crashed to the forest floor, lifeless. His eyes were open, but blank, staring into nothingness. His chest had been ripped apart, and blood and flesh dripped from it. Sharon desperately wanted to throw up.

Then she felt the two eyes of fire turn toward her. "So," the creature mused, "you have spirit. Good. I like a little spirit. He—" she sensed the giant hand pointing at her dead father—"he had pitifully little spirit. But in these miserable days, I take what I can get. A wretched little man like that can hardly satisfy my appetites. . . ." The voice was silent for a moment. "Ah, but once I feasted on many souls. People were flocking to make bargains with me, and I ate very well indeed. And, soon . . ."

The twin fires suddenly materialized in front of her, and she could feel hot, stinking breath from some foul mouth. She tried to turn but was rooted to the spot.

"But you . . ." The voice sighed. "You are a different matter. I can already taste the feast that you will be." It sounded as if he was licking his lips. "I've been waiting for you very patiently. Seventeen years. Seventeen long, hungry years . . ." Suddenly his hand lunged out, and Sharon screamed. She felt the long, ragged talons tearing into her clothes and skin. She was certain that this was the end, but instead, she was released. She staggered back, reeling from the stench of the thing's breath.

She was bruised, hurting, and cut in several places. Her sturdy clothes had been almost shredded to bits. Whimpering in fear, Sharon hunched down, trying to hide. Her knife had been shattered by the blow. She could never fight this monster the way she had faced down Wilde. She was completely at its mercy—and mercy was one thing it didn't possess. The fetid breath played over her, as if the power of darkness was savoring the scent of her fear.

"You were promised to me," the voice told her. "And I shall have you. A pure soul, undiluted by evil. You are mine, Sharon Anders, and I shall come to claim you. . . ." The unseen hand reached out, and she shuddered at its touch. It felt huge, twice the size of a normal hand. Her skin crawled where it rested. "Ah, you will be a true delight."

The fiend laughed. "You beat your father well, child. He will never again be back to haunt you. His soul I have already taken. A pitiful, shriveled husk of a soul, blackened and cheapened by his own excesses and corruptions. One hardly worth the plucking. But you—ah, yours I am looking forward to greatly. . . ."

Sharon tried to move, to run, to do anything. But her terrified body refused to obey her will. She could feel the black pit of death opening under her, ready to swallow her down and destroy her utterly. Again the creature laughed. The hand reached out and pushed her. She tried to fight, but it was useless. The hand pushed her down, pinning her to the dead soil. Something chittered and ran across her face, and she screamed. The immense weight pressed down on her, pushing her into the soil.

Rocks and pebbles tore at her skin and inched under her clothes. Still the pressure increased. The ground slowly gave way as she was physically driven into the soil. She was screaming constantly now, but her struggles were getting weaker and weaker. It was almost impossible for her to breathe.

Soil began to flow over her. It fell into her mouth, choking her. She coughed and tried to vomit it out, but it kept on flowing. It was covering her over, burying her alive. The unseen hand pushed again, and dirt began to force its way up her nostrils. Choking, struggling, she felt the life slipping away from her. She fought, but the coldness, pain, and anguish of death closed all about her. . . .

. . . She woke in utter darkness, with something pressing down on her. Her clothing was in tatters. In a cold wash of fear, she reached upward, hitting a barrier just an inch or so from her face.

She was buried alive!

In panic, she clawed at the wooden lid above her. It was unyielding, and she couldn't get any leverage. Breathing in short spurts, she tried to calm down, but her heart was pounding loudly in her chest. Terror clawed at her soul as she tried to think.

She realized that she couldn't have been buried. There were no side walls that she could feel.

Biting back her terror, she reached out into the darkness and touched something that rustled and moved, like cloth of some kind. . . . Suddenly, comprehension dawned. She wasn't in a coffin—she was under her bed! The weight above her was the bed itself. The cloth was the dust ruffle on the bed. Crawling sideways on her back, she managed to creep out from underneath. Then she sat up, breathing slowly until her heart had slowed to its normal pace once again. In the dim light, she could see that her clothes had been slashed by some huge claw and that there was a web of tiny cuts all over her skin. They itched and tingled, but there was little blood.

How had she gotten under the bed? Had the dream of being pushed into the ground somehow translated into her being pushed right through her bed? It was crazy, but then—so was everything else about this whole affair.

Stiffly, she got to her feet and turned back the bedsheet.

The missing pieces of her clothes were there. They were ripped to tatters, but still in place where she had been sleeping. The fragments of the shattered hunting knife were there, too.

It had been a dream, all right—but the dreams were getting far too real. Who knew—maybe one of these times when she was killed in her nightmare, she would never wake up. . . .

FIFTEEN

Sharon was still shaking in the morning light. After a cautious shower, she dressed for school, then walked slowly downstairs to the breakfast room. She stopped when she saw the table was set—and that several packages were sitting at her place.

"Happy birthday!" her father called out, and her mom echoed his greeting.

Her seventeenth birthday! How could she have forgotten *that*? Struggling to smile and to force down the memories of the night, she walked across to the table. Her parents kissed her, and she tried to concentrate. Open the cards . . . right! That was it. Carefully, Sharon took each envelope and read the messages out loud. In seconds, she had forgotten what they said.

Then she opened the presents. Again, as soon as they were opened, they were gone from her memory. The last one was a certificate for driving lessons, and she did her best to focus on it. Her father was beaming happily at her.

"Pass your test, and we're adding a secondhand car for Christmas," he promised her. "If you're real good, maybe even this Christmas. If we're lucky, you'll be thirty before you pass."

Sharon knew she should be elated, but she simply couldn't summon up the right emotions. She'd been hoping that they would let her take the lessons at school for the longest time, but now, here she was— completely unable to show what this should have meant to her. She ought to be jumping up and down in happiness, but the memories of the nightmare were too vivid.

Eventually, her folks realized that something was wrong. Her father looked at her in concern. "Is something wrong, Shar?"

Sharon shook her head. "Wait a minute," she said, then went upstairs. She came back with a bundle, the wreckage of the previous night. She showed them the shattered knife and the torn clothing, and tried to explain about the nightmare. It turned out to be a mistake. Mr. Anders wouldn't listen to her. He had a more believable explanation in mind, and was furious and afraid for her.

"Some crazy person did this," he snapped, shaking as he held on to the shredded T-shirt. "Somebody who knows you, and is warning you. I'm sorry, Sharon. I should have listened to you before. It's obvious what's been happening now. Some sicko has a fixation on you, and all these weird things have been his way of trying to get your attention. God knows what he might do next. He must be getting into your room somehow at night, and doing all of these things." There were tears in his eyes. "This could have been you he attacked instead of your clothes."

"Dad!" Sharon yelled. "Listen to me! Nobody got into my room last night! At least, not through any normal way. I was wearing those clothes when I fell asleep, and they were like that when I woke up."

"Don't be absurd, Sharon," her father retorted. "It's perfectly clear what's happening. Oh, I should have listened to you all along."

"Then listen to me now," she said, desperately. "It wasn't a maniac. At least, not like you're thinking. It was Johnny Wilde."

Mr. Anders glared at his wife. "I told you that you shouldn't have told her," he snapped.

"*Listen to me!*" Sharon yelled. "It was Johnny Wilde, I know."

"Wilde's dead. He's been dead fifteen years."

"He's dead, all right," Sharon agreed. "And he's gone. The demon he made a deal with killed him for good this time. But it still wants me."

Mr. Anders scowled at his wife. "You even told her about the devil worship, didn't you? I thought you had more sense than that!"

"I didn't!" Mrs. Anders said slowly, staring at Sharon. "I don't know where she got that part from, but it wasn't from me. I never said a word about it."

"Wait a minute," Sharon begged. "What part? What are you talking about?"

Her father looked at her uncertainly. "Well, that a

number of the people in Wilde's commune were into devil worship. Killing chickens, that sort of thing."

Sharon paled. "That's what Wilde wanted me for," she whispered. "I was to be a human sacrifice. He promised me to this demon. My mother—Shanna—wouldn't let him do it. That's why she took me and ran away. Then she led him off so you could find me. When Wilde couldn't deliver me to the demon, the demon killed him."

"That's utter nonsense," Mr. Anders snapped. But he sounded unsure of himself at last.

"It's the only thing that makes sense." Sharon looked from her father to her mother, striving for belief. "Let's face it, it's a lot more likely than Dr. Jablonski's stupid theory, isn't it?"

"Dr. Jablonski?" her father echoed.

"The therapist, dear," Mrs. Anders added.

"I dreamed about her," Sharon said. "That Wilde killed her. And she didn't even believe he was real."

Her father stared at Sharon, then suddenly grabbed the morning paper he'd been skimming and flicked the pages urgently. Finally, he slammed it down on the table, with one page open. "I knew I'd seen it," he said, in a hollow voice. The others followed his shaking finger.

THERAPIST FOUND MURDERED the headline read.

Underneath it was a picture of Dr. Jablonski.

"She was killed a couple of days ago," Mr. Anders said quietly. "When she didn't go to work yesterday morning, the police broke into her house. She'd been murdered in her sleep."

Sharon felt sick, but she forced herself to say:

"And she was wearing a red nightgown, and was stabbed. That's what happened in my dream."

"Don't be foolish," her father said, but he was too nervous to sound angry. He started to scan the page. "You must have heard about it yesterday or something, and thought you'd dreamed it."

"I *did* dream it," Sharon answered. "She wore a red nightgown and was stabbed through the heart, once. It was horrible."

"There's nothing about that in the news story," Mr. Anders muttered. "You're just guessing. You must be. You couldn't possibly know things like that." He sounded as if he was trying to convince himself as much as Sharon.

"Check it," Sharon suggested. "You must know someone at the police department. You're a lawyer. Ask them."

"It's crazy." But her father's voice showed that he was considering it.

"Then prove me wrong," Sharon told him. "If she was wearing something else, or if she wasn't stabbed in the heart, then I'll drop this whole story. I promise. But if she was, you *have* to take me seriously."

Finally, he nodded. He crossed to the kitchen phone and dialed. After a moment, he said: "Hi, Rob. Yeah, it's Henry Anders here. Listen, this Jablonski killing . . . No, not really a professional thing. I don't have a client. Just a funny story. Listen, what was she wearing? Uh-huh? Right . . . And how was she killed, exactly?" He paled at the reply and was so shaken that he hung up without thanking his friend. He slowly poured himself another cup of coffee and sat down. He looked shocked, but told Sharon: "Tell me everything."

As best as she could recall, Sharon told them about her dreams and the threats. She told them about all the bizarre things that had happened. And finally about the demon that had almost appeared to her. Then she sat back and looked at them anxiously.

Both of them were trying very hard not to believe a word of it. But they were too honest to keep it up for long. Finally, her father let out a long breath and shook his head.

"If anyone else was telling me this, I would call the funny farm. It's crazy. But . . . well, you're not a liar, Sharon, and you've never shown any indication that you're a fool, either. It's just . . . well, devils after people's souls isn't exactly twentieth-century thinking, is it?"

"That's not my fault," Sharon answered. "I'm still not really convinced that there are such things as demons, or whatever. But *something* is after me. It's been trying to scare me for weeks now, and it still wants me. It feels that I was promised to it seventeen years ago, and that it has some right to me." She shuddered. "Sort of like an I.O.U. that it's finally going to collect. In blood. My blood."

Mr. Anders shook his head. "I can't believe I'm going along with this." He sighed. "But—well, as crazy as it sounds, your story does kind of hold together. I wish it didn't. If it was just some common or garden maniac, at least I could call up the police for some protection for you. But what can we do about a demon from hell?"

"I don't know." Sharon thought for a moment. "There's just one thing that really puzzles me about all of this."

"Only one thing?" Her mother laughed nervously. "The whole thing puzzles me."

"Well, one thing in particular." Sharon gestured at the newspaper report. "How come Wilde could kill Dr. Jablonski in my dream and have her stay dead in real life? I mean, he's killed me often enough, and I always woke up from it."

"That's part of the reason why I believe you," her father said sadly. "She couldn't wake up. She took sleeping pills. Insane as it sounds, maybe she would have been okay if she could have woken from her dream. But she couldn't . . ."

Sharon shuddered at the thought. "Then," she said, slowly, "there's got to be something else I'm missing out on."

"What do you mean?"

"Well, because I can wake up, there's no point in this demon trying to kill me in my nightmare, is there? But it hasn't given up trying to get me. All it can do is to attack the nonliving things about me. Like the bed, or the paint, or the clothes and knife. But it can't really hurt me."

"I don't know," her mother said. "What about that gash in your arm? That was real enough."

Sharon glanced down at the dressing on her arm. She'd almost forgotten about that. "It must be because I didn't wake up right away. But I *always* wake up when I'm killed in my dream."

Her father nodded. "I think your friend Chiku is right," he told her grimly. "There's another person mixed up in this somewhere. Some living person. Someone who will maybe try to kill you for real."

Nodding, Sharon said: "Chiku felt that there had to be a reason why the demon was attacking me now, and not before. And the demon mentioned having found me again, like he didn't know where I was until recently." She bit at her lip, not wanting to start trouble, but then finally said: "There's this guy at school who's really into horror movies, slasher flicks, that sort of thing. He's really stuck on Chiku. One of the girls said he'd been a Peeping Tom, too."

"You think he might be behind this somehow?" Mr. Anders shrugged. "It's worth a try. I can see if there's any record on him with the police. And find out whatever else I can. What's his name?"

"Larry Wauchop." Sharon felt like she was betraying her friend, but didn't know what else to do. If Larry had decided to make one of his films into reality, maybe he had somehow found out about the old Wilde story? For all she knew, they could even have filmed the story. It was sick enough for that kind of moviemaker. Larry could have seen that film.

"Okay." Her father made a note of the name. "Meanwhile, we should play this safe. You'd better stay home until we sort all of this out, except for school. I'm going to drop you off and pick you up myself. And no going anywhere there aren't plenty of people."

Sharon nodded, then suddenly remembered. "But the Halloween Dance is tomorrow night!"

"Well, that's definitely out," her father said. "It's a costume thing, and anybody might get in."

Disappointment welled up inside her. "But, Dad!" she protested. "It's the highlight of the year. I've got to go! Anyway, I'll be with Chiku and Travis, so I'll be perfectly safe."

"It's too dangerous," her father answered, but a lot less firmly.

"Please," Sharon begged. "I promise, I won't go anywhere unless one of them is with me. I'll be very careful. And after all, I have to cancel a date tonight."

"I'll think about it," he answered. Sharon smiled inwardly. She knew that meant *I'll have to give in, but make it look good.*

"Thanks, Dad," she said, kissing his cheek. "So, are you going to drive me to school now?" She laughed. "Chauffeur service for my birthday!"

Sharon was almost late for class when her father dropped her off at school. Things still seemed very unreal to her, but the fact that her parents were finally taking her nightmares seriously helped a lot.

She saw no sign of Chiku, which puzzled her. Or Larry, for that matter. Maybe he was still acting weird and was avoiding her. Finally, just minutes before the bell, she saw Travis. He waved and came over to her. Before she could cancel their date for that evening, he grimaced.

"I need a rain check," he said. "I'm really sorry,

136

Sharon, but my car's been acting up. Mom had to give me a ride this morning. But I think if I strip the engine down tonight, it'll make it to the dance tomorrow. I definitely don't want to miss that."

"Me neither," Sharon agreed. "And don't worry about tonight. I'm happy we'll be together tomorrow."

He grinned. "Well, in that case I'm going to save your gift for then, too." He gave her a quick peck on the cheek. "Happy birthday."

Still feeling warmed, Sharon sailed into her first class. Chiku was already there.

"I've got news for you," she told Sharon. "But we'd better save it for later." She looked up as Mr. Levine entered the room, ready to begin the art class. Everyone settled down.

After class, Chiku took Sharon aside. "I've got a confession to make," she said, smiling to show it was a good one. "I had to tell my father about your nightmares. He's noticed what I've been researching. I hope you're not mad."

"No," Sharon admitted. "I like your dad, and he's pretty smart."

"Smarter than I like to think." Chiku grinned. "Well, I didn't expect him to believe me—I'm still having a hard time believing it myself sometimes. But he did. He wants to talk to you, and thinks he might be able to help. But he wants to hear the story from you, to make sure he's got all the facts right." She smiled. "He thinks I might have added a bit to your story."

"Did you?"

"Hey, can I help it if I've got an active imagination?" Chiku became suddenly serious. "No, actually, I didn't. He still wants to talk to you. Can you come over for dinner tonight?"

Sharon shrugged. "I'll have to check. I told my folks about the dream, and they're finally starting to take it seriously, too. I'm supposed to be picked up by Dad after school. But he should be happy as long as I'm with you. Hang on, and I'll call him at work."

Her father's secretary put her through so fast that Sharon knew she must have been given instructions to. Her father sounded worried and didn't relax when she asked about going to Chiku's.

"You think that's safe?" he asked.

"Dad, Chiku's my best friend. I've known her for years. And her father is really neat. I'll be safe."

"I hope you're right." He sighed. "Okay, you can go—as long as Mr. Williams will drive you straight home afterward."

As she hung up, Sharon realized that her father was really afraid for her. But she would be with Chiku. There was nothing to worry about.

SIXTEEN

After school, Sharon and Chiku met outside the main building. Chiku was whistling cheerfully to herself. "Guess what?" she asked.

"What?"

"Larry *finally* asked me to the Halloween Dance."

Sharon frowned. "He left it till the last second, didn't he?"

"Better late than never."

"I assume you said yes?" Sharon prompted.

"You bet. I told you, dudette, I was just waiting for him to ask in the right way." Chiku smiled. "He was unusually subdued, and very shy about the whole thing."

"Shy? That doesn't sound like him."

"True. But at least he did it right." Chiku hugged Sharon happily. "I've got a feeling tomorrow night's going to be really memorable for the both of us, girl. You and Travis, me and Larry. What teams!"

Still full of the news, Chiku bubbled on all the

way over to her house. Sharon let it all wash over her, lost in her own thoughts. Maybe Larry wasn't the one behind it all. But—if he was the slasher somehow, was he looking for someone easier now that Sharon had begun to fight back? No, that didn't make sense. The un-man from her nightmares had made it clear that she was the one he was after. So Chiku should be safe. Was Larry's going to the dance just a coincidence? Or, if he was the killer, was he going to do something there?

Questions spun around in her head, but she didn't have the answers to them. All she could do was to play it very carefully from now on.

Sharon liked Chiku's parents. Mr. Williams was a kind, somewhat dry man who taught at the local college. Mrs. Williams was a cheerful secretary, sort of like a subdued older version of her daughter. Both were always happy to see Sharon, who they considered a "good influence" on Chiku. ("Little do they know . . ." Chiku would whisper.)

After dinner, Mr. Williams took the two girls into his study. It was a comfortable room, well stocked with books, papers, and magazines that he used for his notes and research. Volumes on folklore, mythology, and the occult littered the place. When they had been younger, Chiku had borrowed some of the books to read ghost stories for her slumber parties. They had always sent shudders through Sharon.

Indicating that they should sit on the slightly beat-up old sofa, Mr. Williams picked up one of the pipes from his crowded desk and bit on the end of it. He had given up smoking after being nagged for years by his wife and daughter, but he always concentrated better when he had a pipe—even an unlit one—firmly between his teeth. Then he asked Sharon to tell him the whole story.

She did so, leaving out as little as she could. Though she felt uncomfortable, she even included the therapist's theory that she was simply afraid of sex. When she was finished, she sat quietly and waited. Mr. Williams nodded slowly to himself, lost in a maze of thoughts. Finally, he stirred and unfolded from the chair he was lounging in.

"It's a remarkable story," he offered.

"You don't believe me," Sharon said, embarrassed.

"On the contrary." He stood up and took down one of his thick, old books. "What you've told me makes perfect sense, given a firm understanding of the lore of demonology. Which I know you don't possess." He smiled seriously at her. "Otherwise I'd think you were making it up. No, I believe you completely." He placed the pipe back on his desk. "I'm a little dazed by the opportunity that you present. A genuine supernatural experience that I can study is a dream come true for me."

"I'm pretty tired of dreams coming true," Sharon said.

"I'm sure you are," Mr. Williams assured her.

"Then you do believe me," Sharon said, glad she didn't have to argue her case before another skeptical adult.

"I'm a rational man, Sharon, and I prefer Occam's Razor."

"What?"

"Occam's Razor. It's an old proverb, but a true one. He was a philosopher who said that the simplest answer is usually the right one. In the case of your story, I've considered all of the possible alternatives." He started to tick them off on his fingers. "One, you're lying. That doesn't make sense. Why would you bother? For attention? You've got as much as you can deal with, I think. Besides, I've known you for years, and you've always been at least as truthful as most girls your age ever are. Two, you're crazy. That it's all in your head. I don't buy that. I can't explain the death of the therapist and the other incidents so glibly, and you certainly sound perfectly sane to me. Three, you're mistaken. Maybe the whole thing is just a string of coincidences, and you've put them together in a pattern in your mind. That would make sense if I were willing to accept a great number of coincidences. And if I knew you already knew a lot of demonology. But again, you don't, and I'm not.

"Which only leaves me with: Four, you're telling the truth as you see it." Mr. Williams started to hunt for the pipe that he'd placed on his desk. When he couldn't find it, he picked up another and put that in his mouth. "So—where does that leave us?"

"I don't know," Sharon admitted, miserably. "I really wish one of the other answers was what we were left with, though."

"Believe me, so do I. But we have to accept the fact that there does seem to be some . . . entity, some power out there that wants you." He tapped the book he had selected. "For the sake of argument, let's call it a demon. Some nonphysical creature that somehow has a taste for human souls."

"All this theory is fine," Chiku interrupted. "But we don't want to *study* it. We want to get rid of it, and help Sharon."

"Slow down, honey. You're always so impatient." He smiled at her fondly. "Let's take this one step at a time." Mr. Williams focused on Sharon again. "Demons are traditionally the remnants of the fallen angels. Powers of good, twisted and corrupted by their rebellion against God and thrown down into hell forever as a punishment." He shrugged. "That's the idea, anyway. Actually, what tends to happen is that when a religion takes root in a community, it generally displaces an older faith. The gods of the old faith tend to become the devils of the new. Still, the one thing that all of the theories agree on is that these demons or whatever do have immense powers. But they're constrained by the powers of good and can't simply use their abilities as they wish. Though they can act against the innocent, they generally do so through some human agent. And to work through an agent, they usually have some sort of agreement or contract with him or her."

"A sort of pact with the devil?" suggested Sharon.

"Exactly. I'm not certain what sort of form it takes, but it's generally very businesslike. The demon promises the human something the human is after, like power or wealth, or long life, and in return the demon usually gets the human's soul."

Chiku snorted. "It doesn't sound like much of a deal to me."

"True." Mr. Williams chewed at his pipe. "Sometimes, the humans can get away with their own souls and promise something else. Of course, if they fail to deliver, there's a clause in their contract that says they have to pay a penalty."

Sharon shuddered. "Like their own souls. Wilde had to pay when he couldn't sacrifice me to this demon."

"Exactly," Mr. Williams agreed. "He promised you, and when he failed, the demon collected the penalty—Wilde's soul, to torture and devour. But the demon didn't really want Wilde—he wanted you, and apparently still does."

"But *why*? What could this thing want with me?"

Changing the subject slightly, Mr. Williams said: "The original concepts of the demons of the underworld are very interesting. The demons were originally angels, creatures of beauty and light. Then they rebelled against God and were thrown out of heaven and cast into the pits of hell. On the way down, their original light and beauty were lost, and they became misshapen things, hating and fearing anything good and pure."

Chiku shrugged. "So what? What's this got to do with Sharon?"

"Well, oh impatient daughter, I'm getting to that." He pointed at Sharon with his pipe stem. "The demons hate any form of beauty, especially moral beauty. They hate it with a passion, and they seek to either destroy or contaminate it. Traditionally, they seek the sacrifice of a firstborn child because the child is pure and innocent. Killing it is their way of destroying that innocence. And if they can't destroy it, they love to seduce it over to evil, to corrupt it. I think that this demon that Wilde made the bargain with still wants to corrupt you utterly, Sharon. You're a good kid, and this makes you appealing as a target. It's trying to hurt and terrify you first, and then it will have you as a sacrifice."

Shuddering, Sharon nodded. "I guess it makes some kind of twisted sense. But I'm not the pure and innocent kid you think. I've done enough wrong things in my life, believe me."

Mr. Williams laughed. "I'm not saying you're a saint! I'm certain that you've told lies, dodged responsibilities, and so forth. But compared to the utter blackness of a demon's spirit, almost any human soul is like a searchlight beam. Only humans who accept evil unconditionally into themselves could possibly be less. I'm certain you're good enough to be a very tempting target for this demon that's after you. But it's not that simple."

"What do you mean?" Chiku asked, puzzled.

"Well," her father said, putting his hand on her shoulder, "as much trouble as you are, I have to admit you're probably just as attractive in spiritual terms to a demon as Sharon is. So why did it pick Sharon?"

"Because I was promised to it once," Sharon said.

"Exactly. Wilde promised you as a human sacrifice to this demon. It still sees you as legitimate prey. Like I said, demons are very legalistic. They have everything in a contract. Wilde promised you as payment, and it aims to collect."

"Terrific." Sharon sighed. "I'm some sort of human I.O.U."

Mr. Williams nodded. "And it has somehow found you again after all these years. There can only be one explanation: Someone else has made a contract with it, allowing it access to the human world again. And while it was here, it saw you."

"Chiku said that it was probably someone I know," Sharon said slowly. "Probably someone at school."

"That makes sense."

"Then it has to be someone I met since the beginning of this year. That's when the dreams started."

"Not necessarily." Mr. Williams replaced the pipe in his mouth. "It could also be someone you've known for a long time, who's only recently made a pact with this same demon. It's not bound to be the *human* who found you recently—if that person had just made a pact with the demon this summer, say, then the demon could only have had access to you from that point."

"Then it could be anybody at all," Sharon complained, disappointed with losing what looked like a promising lead.

"No, not at all," he answered. "Anyone who makes a deal with a demon has made a conscious decision to become evil. In which case, that person is bound to be affected by their inner evil. So you can probably eliminate anyone who behaves consistently in a good fashion. I'm certain that this contact is hiding his or her identity and real inclinations as best they can, but sooner or later the mask they're wearing will slip, and it'll show through. You simply have to be alert, and careful."

Chiku objected: "That's all assuming we've got plenty of time. But that demon killed Wilde off for good last night. It seems to be getting pretty impatient. I bet Sharon doesn't have that long before the looney tries to get her for real. Isn't there any way we can trap him or expose him?"

Mr. Williams nodded, slowly. "There are always ways. But they become more and more dangerous. For example, we could try to summon up the demon ourselves. But that isn't a real safe thing to try. Like I said, demons are bound by the powers of goodness. They can't actually harm humans directly. Sharon's demon can't just kill her himself. He needs a human agent to do it. But if we called him up, we'd give him power, and demons can use that power against you. Anyway, we would need to know the name of the demon to be able to call him up. And we don't have the slightest idea of what it might be. If you know its name, you have a little bit of control. Without it, you're stuck."

Sharon thought for a moment, then said: "Well, how about an exorcism?"

"You've been watching too many movies. An exorcism only dispels a spirit or demon from a person or place. But you're not the one that the demon has taken over. We'd have to find out who the human agent is first to do that. So we're back where we started." Then he smiled. "Still, you have given me one idea." He shot around the desk and began to rummage through the drawers. Finally he emerged, holding something in his hand. "Here, wear this."

He held it out, and Sharon took it. It was an ornate cross, about two inches tall, on a silver chain. She looked at him, puzzled.

"It's a silver crucifix," he explained. "It was given to me by a bishop a few years ago. Not the sort of thing I usually wear, but perfect as a defense for you. While you're wearing that, the demon will have to stay back."

"Like good magic?" asked Sharon. She pulled it over her head. It hung down just inside the front of her shirt.

"Actually, no," Mr. Williams answered. "In and of itself, that's just a nice and fairly expensive piece of jewelry. But what it does is to concentrate in your mind the beliefs and strengths of goodness. That cross has no power unless you have goodness in your soul. It concentrates your own beliefs and strengths into an image, if you like. But that should be enough to hold off the demon. They can't stand anything pure. That's why it tries to terrify you. Fear is a strong negative emotion, and it gives the demon something to latch on to to attack you." He held up a warning hand. "But that cross will only help against the demon. It won't work against people. You see, while demons are bound to certain laws which they must obey, human beings are much freer. They can do as they please and choose either good or evil as they want. Don't be fooled into thinking that cross will burn an evil human being. It doesn't work like that."

Sharon struggled to understand. "But it sounds like it'll help me at least a bit."

"Certainly. And we can use all the help that we can get. So wear it all the time—even in bed and in the shower. It will focus your mind on good, instead of leaving you open to attack."

"It's not coming off until I'm safe," Sharon promised.

"Good." Mr. Williams stretched. "Well, that's about all we can do for now. I'll give you a ride home. Keep a lookout for anyone who might be the human agent for this demon. Remember, however hard they might try to hide it, if they've sold out to a demon, their inner evil will have to show itself." He glanced at his daughter. "It wouldn't hurt you to keep your own eyes open, either."

"I might spot something Sharon misses, eh?" Chiku looked smug.

"No," her father answered. "But this agent is already planning a human sacrifice. I'm worried that he or she would hurt you if you were in the way. So be very careful. Both of you."

Brushing her hair for bed that night didn't take very long. Sharon still hated her hair short, but at least it was easier to manage. As she stared at her own reflection, brushing away, she could see the light flashing off the crucifix around her neck. It made her feel safer just to have it there.

All in all, it hadn't been such a bad day, she reflected. Maybe she hadn't had her date with Travis, but she did finally have some hope at last. Her parents believed her story—and so did Chiku's dad. That helped a lot, knowing there were adults who didn't think she was crazy, or imagining things.

In fact, her father was taking her very seriously. He'd nailed her bedroom window shut, to stop anyone getting to her that way. He'd called an alarm company, who had promised they could install a house security system by the end of the week. He'd even insisted on checking the closet for her before she went to bed. Her mother had offered to spend the night with her, but Sharon had turned her down. Partly because she didn't want to be a wimp, but mostly because if the demon did try anything, not only would her mother not be able to help, but she could be in danger, too. Sharon had left her bedroom door ajar, and the hall light was on. Just in case she started to call out in her sleep.

Sharon had shown her parents the crucifix that Mr. Williams had given her. Mrs. Anders had thought it was a good idea, and had insisted on getting her old rosary beads out and hanging them on the hook on Sharon's door. Mrs. Anders had said firmly: "I'd rather take precautions that we don't need than not take precautions that we do need." Sharon had given in, but she felt like she was living in a war zone.

And perhaps she was, at that.

She was glad that Travis had canceled their date, after all. What would he think of her if he knew what was happening? Would he dump her, thinking she was crazy? After all, maybe she was putting him in danger, too, simply by knowing him. Maybe it'd be better not to see him at all until the demon finally left her alone.

Selfishly, she didn't want to do that. Travis was one good thing that had happened to her lately. Besides, how long would she have to go on living looking over her shoulder? When could she know she was safe?

Unwanted, another dreadful thought crept into her mind: *Maybe Travis is behind this?*

She tried to force it out, but it wasn't that simple. How could she possibly suspect him? He was the kindest, gentlest person she'd ever known, and he had shown that he cared about her. It was terrible even to consider the possibility that he was behind this.

But he came into your life when the dream did, the insinuating voice whispered to her. *Do you really think that's a coincidence?*

No, she was certain Travis couldn't be the human agent of any demon. Mr. Williams had said that anyone who was linked to a demon would have to show his evilness. And Travis simply wasn't like that. She'd still put her money on Larry—he gave her the creeps.

Sharon slipped into bed and turned out the light. Despite everything, she still felt worried. She had a strong feeling that the demon wasn't going to give up on her yet.

Sharon drifted into sleep. And, for the first time in days, her dreams were all peaceful.

SEVENTEEN

Friday was one of those endless days when it seemed like school would never be over. The teachers knew that the students were focusing on the dance that evening, but nevertheless attempted to achieve some small level of education. It all flew past Sharon. The thought of going to the dance with Travis almost made up for the terrible nights she'd been through.

It was strange how attracted to him she had become. She had never really believed in the old "love at first sight" theory, but there wasn't any other way to explain what had happened to her. Travis seemed to set her emotions on fire, and she felt warm just thinking about his name or his handsome face.

Finally, though, the day was over. Her father had wanted to take her over to Travis's house himself, but then a big case finally broke, and he had to be in court for an arraignment. Chiku arranged to pick her up at seven and then drop her at Travis's house. Mr. Anders had finally, reluctantly, given in. He was still unhappy with the thought of Sharon attending the dance at all, but he knew she was completely determined to go.

After school, Chiku shot home to get her costume ready. At her own home, Sharon picked dreamily through her dinner, then went upstairs to change for the dance.

Her mother had suggested that Sharon go as a black cat. Sharon couldn't come up with a better idea, and had agreed. At least it was an easy costume. She put on the long-sleeved black leotard and black tights, then admired the effect in the mirror. Mrs. Anders had made a black headband with pointy ears, and a long black tail as well. She had to admit that she looked pretty cute. *Very slinky.* Black eyeliner whiskers were the finishing touch.

"You look adorable, honey," her mother said. "Very Halloween."

"Meow," Sharon replied, then laughed.

Downstairs, she waited impatiently for Mr. Williams to arrive to pick her up, alternating between watching the driveway and the clock. "Come on, come on," she muttered until the lights of a car showed, and she was out of the door almost before Mr. Williams had started to honk his horn.

Chiku—dressed in a long green robe and fairytale pointed hat—started giggling at the sight of Sharon. "This is going to be some fun evening," she said. "Me as Maid Marian, and you as the local mousecatcher. A black outlaw and a black cat!"

Soberly, Mr. Williams added: "But I hope you haven't taken off that crucifix."

Suddenly serious again, Sharon pulled it up out of the neck of her leotard. "I'm keeping it on till I know I'm safe," she promised.

"Good." Mr. Williams backed out of the driveway and set off across town. "Now, where does Travis live again?"

"Willowbrook Estates," Chiku said.

"Isn't that the new development on the edge of town?" her father asked.

"Uh huh. Travis only moved in in September. One of the first houses there. They're still building the rest."

"Expensive, if I remember right." Mr. Williams grinned at Sharon. "You've got expensive tastes, it seems."

"I only want the best." She laughed. "Like Chiku for a friend."

"You're just saying that," Chiku snorted, but she was obviously happy with the compliment.

The drive was about fifteen minutes, but they finally pulled into the suburb. As Chiku had said, there were only half a dozen houses completed. The site was at the edge of Willowbrook Woods, and a swath into the trees had already been cut for the next stage of developments.

The houses were large, and clearly in the quarter-of-a-million-dollar range at least. Sharon directed Mr. Williams to the address Travis had given her. It was the farthest house from the main road.

Chiku whistled. "His parents have got to be loaded! Girl, you are definitely doing all right here!"

"You're so mercenary." Sharon sighed theatrically. "I like Travis for *himself.*"

"Yeah, right." Chiku grinned. "Okay, out. We still have to pick up my date."

"Okay." Sharon hopped out of the car, careful to pull her tail out with her. "See you in a while."

Mr. Williams wished her a good night, but didn't start the car until he saw the door to the house open and Sharon wave back before she went in. Then he breathed easier and drove off.

"Where does this Larry live again?"

Chiku shook her head. "I don't know how you manage to teach anyone anything," she complained. "You can't remember an address for ten straight minutes."

"I use a lot of notes," he answered.

Travis met Sharon at the door and gave her an admiring look. "Great costume," he told her. "You're the prettiest kitten I've seen all day."

Sharon curtsied and smiled. "Thank you, kind sir." Then, seriously, she asked: "Did you get the car fixed?"

"Oh, sure. It's going fine now." He smiled, slow and easy. "I've just got to get my own things ready. It won't take long. Why don't you wait in Mom's study?" He led her down the hallway and opened one of the doors. Reaching inside, he switched on the light. "I'll be back in a second."

"I'll be waiting," she promised. As Travis headed upstairs, she glanced around the room. Whatever Mrs. Hale did for a living, she clearly made lots of money from it. Sharon didn't know much about antiques, but the Tiffany lamps alone were probably worth a small fortune. She wondered if Mrs. Hale was married, widowed, or divorced. Travis had never spoken about his father. Still, they hadn't known each other that long, and there were plenty of things they still had to learn.

Sharon started to browse around the room, making her way slowly toward the large oak desk by the French windows. The shades were still open, and she could see that outside was a large backyard and an in-ground pool. Beyond that was a fringe of darkness, where the woods began.

That brought her dream suddenly to mind, and she shuddered. Then she firmly fought down her memories. This was not a night for nightmares. It was for laughter and—hopefully!—romance. . . .

Chiku was stunned when she saw Larry approaching the car. Her father sat, equally speechless. Whatever else was to be said about him, Larry hadn't skimped on his costume. He'd probably get a prize for it, but . . .

"How do you like it?" Larry's voice was muffled inside the full Godzilla face mask. His body was even less recognizable inside the full suit, the green scales, the spiked spine, and the long tail that bounced jauntily in the air behind him. He was the Japanese movie monster in almost perfect miniature.

"It's very impressive," Mr. Williams finally managed to say.

"Dad's got a friend who makes these things in

Hollywood," Larry explained. "Completely authentic."

"It must be hard to walk in it," Chiku said.

"Yeah, a little," Larry agreed.

"Then how do you expect to *dance* in it?" she asked, with a touch of impatience in her voice.

"Oh." Larry was quiet for a moment. "Right, this is a dance, isn't it?" He looked down at himself. "I guess this really wasn't the best choice, then."

He sounded so disappointed that Chiku relented. "Look, why don't you just wear it to make a grand entrance, and then take the mask and tail off so you can at least shake it up with me?"

"Okay," he agreed. "Umm . . . Maybe I should take the tail off now? I don't know if I can sit down with it on."

When Larry finally managed to get in the backseat, Chiku broke out in giggles, seeing him sitting there, clutching his detached tail in his paws. "This is going to be a wild evening," she said as her dad pulled away from the curb. "Still, that's what I get for dating a guy who's into schlocky horror pics."

Larry squirmed. "Well, to be honest . . ." He paused, and then said, almost in a single breath: "I'm not really into those slasher movies, actually. They're kind of sick, you know? But I thought it was cooler to like them, and I kinda felt that people treated me better if they thought I liked them."

"Ah, youth," Mr. Williams muttered. "Image over truth every day." He caught the filthy look his daughter flashed him, and added: "So, what sort of movies do you really like, then?"

"Really?" Larry was embarrassed. "Well, I love Disney stuff."

"You do?" Chiku bounced up. "What's your favorite? Mine's *The Little Mermaid*."

"It is?" Sounding surprised that he wasn't being laughed at, Larry said: "Mine's *The Great Mouse Detective*."

"Maybe if you invited me over to watch one of *them*, I'd say yes," Chiku hinted with all the subtlety of a brick thrown through a window.

"Yeah. That's what Travis said," Larry told her. "He is the one who told me to just ask you to the dance like a normal person." Larry frowned and scratched his neck with one claw.

"Well, I'm glad you listened to him."

Larry laughed, somewhat bitterly. "Listened? Oh, I listened all right. How else do you think I got that black eye?"

Chiku frowned, puzzled. "You don't mean that Travis punched you?"

"Yup. He was very convincing," Larry said dryly.

"That doesn't make sense," Chiku said slowly. "Why would he beat you up to make you be nice to me? It doesn't sound like him."

Snorting, Larry said: "Then you've been taken in by his cute face and slick manners. Believe me, the guy's a jerk. He didn't want me to take you out because he was being nice to you. He just didn't want you around to ruin his date with Sharon tonight. And he told me to make good and certain of that, or he'd break my arm next time." Larry shivered. "I

158

almost think he meant it. He gave me a ride home in his car tonight, and made sure that I'd asked you."

"Tonight?" Chiku frowned. "But he told Sharon that his car was still being fixed."

"Listen, I don't want to upset you," Larry answered, "but I think he's been lying to her. A lot. He'd say anything to get her to do what he wants. He's a real creep."

A feeling of shock and fear started spreading through Chiku's body. She glanced at her father and Mr. Williams jammed on the brakes, and, oblivious to the angry horn of the car behind him, turned around to stare at Larry's Godzilla face.

"What exactly did he say about Chiku?"

"Er—something about *'I don't want that Williams girl around to spoil my plans for Sharon.'* You know, I think he's going to try and put a move on her, and didn't want Chiku around to stop him."

"I don't think a 'move' is what he has in mind," Mr. Williams said grimly, confirming the terror that Chiku was feeling. He put the car in gear again, and turned it around. "Look out for a phone, will you? We've got to call and warn her."

"Then you think . . ." Chiku couldn't finish the sentence.

"Yes," her father agreed. "I think Travis has finally made his mistake and revealed his true colors. He's the one who's hunting Sharon."

Larry looked at both of them in complete bewilderment. "Is there something I don't know about?" he asked plaintively.

EIGHTEEN

Sharon paused by the desk and admired the beautiful stained-glass lamp there. It was of interconnected dragonflies and seemed very old. Then, as she was looking at it, the open scrapbook on the desk's blotter caught her eye.

There were photos in it, and clippings. Feeling a little nosy and guilty, she circled the desk to examine the open pages of the thick volume. There were two photos, both of paintings. The first was of what looked like out-of-focus flowers. Under it was a neat label: STILL LIFE, BY TAMAR HALE. Obviously Travis's mother. The other was a similar piece, KERIOG'S PROMISE. It was hard to identify, but seemed to be some sort of inverted rainbow, with a pot of gold at the bottom of it. She wasn't into modern art and had no idea what either meant.

The clipping was about an exhibition of the works of Tamar Hale. The article had a picture of her by another painting. Sharon could see where

Travis had gotten his dark good looks, because his mother was really gorgeous. Then, as she skimmed the piece, thinking how nice it was that his mother was so talented, she froze. Then she reread the last line:

"At one time, Ms. Hale was a member of the now defunct Lost Arts Community of Paineston, PA."

Wilde's group . . .

Hardly daring to breathe, and not wanting to think, Sharon blindly turned the page. There were just two large photos on those pages, and she recognized them both. The first was of Wilde himself, the lopsided, sadistic smile on that face, so familiar from her nightmares. On the other page was the painting she had seen in the recent dream, the streaks of angry red and black. It was labeled KERIOG'S NOTHING. The redness seemed more like blood than ever.

She backed away from the book, blindly looking around. Travis's mother had been one of Wilde's coworkers at the Paineston colony. . . . And she was here, now. Travis had arrived at the same time that the nightmares had begun. . . . And the demon had said that he had just recently found her again.

"Travis . . ." she breathed, unwilling to really believe it.

"Yes," he said, from the doorway. "Travis."

Sharon startled and looked up, and Travis smiled at the fear in her eyes. "I knew that if I left you long enough, you'd figure it out. Well, at least some of it, anyway."

"You," she said, pointing a shaky finger at him. "You're the one the demon's using to try to get me."

Travis smiled again. Sharon could see nothing romantic or appealing in the smile now. It was filled with bitterness and viciousness, just like Wilde's had been. How could she have been so stupid, so utterly blind to the truth?

"Yeah, I'm the one who told on you," he agreed. He sauntered slowly across the room until he stood on the far side of the desk from her. He glanced down at the open scrapbook. "Oh, you didn't finish. Turn the page."

Hardly knowing what she'd find, Sharon numbly obeyed. One side of the page was blank, but there was evidence that a clipping was missing. On the other side she saw some headlines, and the picture of her dead mother again.

"I had to use the other one that night for your dream," he told her. "To start you on the way to learning the truth. But I knew exactly who you were the first time I saw you at school." He smiled. "And I knew what to do about it."

"Why?" Sharon asked, feeling all her hopes, her fantasies, and her dreams crashing about her. "Why? How could you do what you did?"

His smile was starting to get on her nerves now. All of the goodness and kindness she had seen—or imagined—in him was completely gone. In its place was the studied gaze of an animal staring at a deer it was about to kill. "My mother kept that book for years," he told her. "I read it from cover to cover dozens of times. She told me all about Johnny Wilde, all the stuff that isn't in any of the newspapers. Plenty that nobody else knows." He looked really smug now, and she knew he was setting her up for another shock. "Not even you, even though you met him in your worst nightmares."

Keeping the desk between them, Sharon couldn't help glancing at the phone on the desk. Travis saw her look, and laughed. "Try it," he said. "It's dead. There's no help for you now. We're all alone. Mom's out of town at a gallery show, and your friends are all busy at the dance." He laughed. "And your stepfather is busy in court. You know, he called me up earlier, to ask me to be sure to take real good care of you. I promised that I would. But—don't you want to hear the rest?"

While he was still talking, there was time for something—anything—to happen. Sharon nodded. Travis smiled again, secure in his own strength and planning.

"She told me about his pact with the demon. That it promised him power, wealth, fame . . . All he had to do was to sacrifice his firstborn child to it."

"Me . . ."

"You," he agreed cheerfully. "But Wilde was weak, and he made mistakes. Your mother got away with you, and he failed. As a result, he paid the penalty."

Sharon nodded. None of this was news. She wanted Travis to get on with the story—and she also wanted him to stretch it out as long as possible, to give her time to think.

"Well, I made a deal with the same demon," Travis told her. "I called him up, just like Wilde did. He offered me the same deal, on the same terms. I get to have power, money, fame—anything I like. And all I have to do to get them, is to kill you."

Sharon's mouth was dry. She could feel her heart pounding, and she wanted to scream. But she knew that to survive this conversation she had to keep her head. Forcing her panic back down, she simply stared at him. He could read the contempt and disgust in her eyes, and she could see that it didn't bother him at all. Smiling, he raised his right hand above the level of the desk.

He was holding the art knife.

Sharon began to shake uncontrollably. Cruelly, Travis laughed again and turned the knife slowly under her mesmerized stare. "Yes, I took the knife. This knife is going to paint a pretty little picture of death—on you. . . ." Then he stopped. "But there is one last little thing I haven't told you, isn't there? Would you like to hear it?"

It was getting harder and harder for Sharon to keep her terror under any kind of control now. She simply wanted to scream, to run, to do anything but stand there and listen to Travis. But she managed to force herself to nod.

"I thought you might." His smile was dazzling now. "Wilde was your father—and I'm your brother." He laughed now. "Your half brother, actually. Just a few weeks younger than you. I guess I lucked out in that. A couple of weeks earlier, and our positions would be reversed, wouldn't they?"

Her half brother . . . Sharon had often wondered what it would be like if she had brothers or sisters, instead of being an only child. Now that she knew she had a brother, she felt sick and disgusted. And repulsed, remembering the romantic fantasies she'd had about him. "No," she managed to croak. "No, they wouldn't. Because I'd never make a deal with a devil to kill anyone."

He looked at her and nodded. "That's right. You're too goody-goody for that, aren't you? Well, I'm not." He raised the knife again. "In fact, I'm really going to enjoy myself."

"You're crazy," she said, desperately trying to think of anything she could do. "You know, Chiku and her father know I came here. If I don't turn up at the dance, they'll come looking for me. You can't do anything to me here."

"Can't I?" he asked, still amused. "My darling big sister, you're so naive. Once I kill you, I will be granted whatever I want. There's no way anyone will be able to prosecute me for your death. My demon won't allow it." He thought for a moment. "Actually, that would be pretty fun—to have everybody know I killed you, but be totally unable to do a thing about it."

"You really are insane, aren't you?" Sharon realized that he was completely consumed by his plans. Killing her would mean nothing to him. It was purely a business transaction.

He shrugged. "Think what you want," he told her. "It doesn't matter. Your life is almost finished now."

"No!" she screamed, finally breaking. The panic inside her welled up, and, hardly knowing what she was doing, she snatched up the scrapbook and hurled it straight into his face.

With a curse, Travis tried to shield himself, but the edge of the book clipped him over the eye and smacked his head backward. He staggered, but didn't fall, as the book thumped onto the thick carpet. Travis glared at her, and Sharon saw that the book had gashed him just over the right eye, and that blood was trickling down his face. He looked down at the back of his hand where his own blood was smeared, and snarled. Every vestige of his false humor was gone, and she saw only death in his eyes.

There was no escape past him. Sharon whirled and fumbled at the French doors behind her. They were locked. Through the glass, she could see the garden, so close, yet unreachable.

"You idiot," he snarled, and lunged for her across the desk. Sharon screamed as the knife raked her left forearm, leaving a bloody trail of pain behind it. But Travis didn't have quite enough reach. As he stretched to his fullest, his face a mask of fury, Sharon snatched the Tiffany lamp and smashed it down on his arm, hard.

The glass shattered, and he howled in pain. She could see more of his blood, this time soaking into the blotter. He jerked back his hand, tearing shards of shattered glass out of his flesh, leaving the bright redness of blood.

Before Travis could attack her again, Sharon spun around and kicked the desk chair toward the windows as hard as she could. It hit the glass, exploding it outward into the night. Heedless of the risk of cutting herself, she hurled herself out of the opening and onto the inviting lawn. She heard Travis swear again and start around the desk after her.

She paused just long enough to take a breath, and then she ran.

The fear within her was eating at her strength and courage. The final stage of her nightmare was real at last. This time the killer would not stop until she was dead—really and truly dead.

Sharon sped around the dark hole that was the pool, then the lawn simply stopped, and she was in the trees. The darkness closed about her, and the branches whipped at her face as she staggered through the night.

NINETEEN

Sharon ran on as the ground rose slightly under her feet. She could hardly see where she was going, and the continuous slapping of branches against her arms hurt and cut into her. Half-panting, half-sobbing, she kept going as best she could.

It was much, much worse than any of her nightmares. She was aware of the heavy, clinging scent of the soil, the intense, burning pain of each breath drawn into her heaving lungs. The night was still, with no sounds that she herself wasn't making in her blind flight. No chance at all of help.

How far could she go? She didn't know how big these woods were, or if she might suddenly break through to a road or someone's backyard. But then, for all she knew, she might even be running in a circle. Without light, it was impossible to tell.

Pausing, Sharon leaned against a tree, listening for the sound of pursuit. She knew that Travis was after her. But there was nothing to hear apart from her own labored breathing. Her body was already tired, and it was all she could do to start moving again. She just wanted to collapse, but that would be fatal. And she was already as awake as she would ever be.

How could she have been so stupid? She knew that the answer was simple: She had deluded herself. Travis's smile, his dark good looks, his friendly—no, affectionate—manner . . . She had wanted to be taken in by them, and she had been. She had wanted Travis to be her knight—and instead he was her nightmare.

She staggered, and fell to one knee on the rough ground. She felt a sharp rock rip her tights and break her skin, sending a fresh lance of pain through her tortured body. If she had only picked a costume with pants! Or a weapon . . . But wishes were useless now. Dragging herself upright, she winced at the stab of pain in her knee. She started onward again, but each step was agony. Clutching her knee, she could feel the blood welling out.

Damn! Of all the times to be so clumsy . . . She collapsed onto the ground and tugged at the torn stocking. After a few tries, she succeeded in ripping off enough material for a compress. Using her headband, she managed to wrap it around her knee. Hopefully that would keep it from bleeding too badly, and enable her to go on. The parallel between this event and her nightmare was chilling. How much more would come true this night?

Sharon stood up and started off again. The knee still hurt, but it didn't seem to be quite as bad as before. Limping and wincing with pain, she moved as fast as she could. But to where? What chance did she have?

She rubbed at her eyes to remove the tears that were forming. She was furious with herself. This was no time to wimp out! This was—

She ran headfirst smack into a branch in the darkness. The searing pain in her forehead almost eclipsed the pain in her body as she fell to the ground. Whimpering in pain and panic, she tried to get up again, but it was no use. She was simply too exhausted to even stagger to her feet.

Panting heavily, she managed to drag herself to the trunk of the tree and leaned back against the bark. Her every breath was almost a cough, and she could taste blood inside her mouth. She must have bitten her lip. Whatever she had done, it was such a minor pain that she couldn't even identify it. Her lungs burned and her throat hurt. Her forehead was already swelling from the blow, and she couldn't focus her eyes. Her knee was a dull throbbing agony. In fact, there wasn't much on her body that didn't hurt her in one way or another.

How long did she dare rest? How far behind was Travis? Sharon shook her head in an effort to clear it. It never occurred to her that she might have lost him in the darkness. She knew better than that.

A faint breeze touched her hair. She brushed it back and caught the smell on the air. It was rotting flesh—faint, but clear. She felt sickened but fought back her nausea. She couldn't be weak now. . . . She peered through the darkness back the way she had come. Was it her imagination, or was there a faint, wavering light far off in the trees?

Then she knew what it was. The demon was here.

Her heart racing, Sharon's fresh terror gave her the strength to regain her feet. Arms outstretched to fend off further collisions, she stumbled onward through the blackness. Travis alone was bad enough, but of course the demon wanted to be in on the kill.

Coughing and wheezing with the agony of each breath, Sharon kept going as long as she could. All of her pains melted into one single, huge mass of throbbing pain that was her body. She refused to think, refused to panic, refused to do anything but run.

Finally, she had to stop. A slight upward slope was more than she could take. Losing her footing, she half-slid, half-fell down a small embankment into the cold trickle of a ditch. Giddily, she tried to get up, but couldn't. As the world of blackness above her spun, she sighed and collapsed, completely drained.

After a few moments, Sharon's head started to clear slightly. The pain in her body was numbing to a level she could stand, and she began to realize where she was. First of all, she was on her back in a shallow stream of chilly water. It was no more than an inch deep, but the back of her head, back, and shoulders were wet and cold. Screwing up her remaining strength, she rolled onto her hands and knees, then rocked back on her heels. Water trickled down the back of her leotard.

Something she had disturbed ran across her left

leg. Shuddering, she didn't even have the strength to bat it away. Tiny legs scuttled across her cold flesh, and then there was a tiny splash as it dived off. She didn't want to know what it might have been.

Using the back of her left hand, she managed to brush dirt and filthy water from around her mouth and eyes. With effort her tired eyes finally managed to focus.

On Travis.

He was standing there, watching her, on the bank of the tiny stream. The knife in his hand was raised, held out in front of him.

"Surprise," he murmured.

Fear rose in her, and she tried to clamber to her feet. But her knees wouldn't take the strain, and she fell back.

"Don't worry," Travis said mockingly. "Soon you'll be able to rest. For a long, long time . . ."

Sharon winced, and he laughed, drinking in her terror and exhaustion. Then he began to move slowly toward her.

Sharon felt suddenly almost supernaturally aware of everything at that moment. She was still watching Travis approach her, but it was as if she were also seeing another layer of reality superimposed upon the woods. She could finally see the demon, as it stood, watching and waiting for her fresh blood.

It glowed slightly from some sickly inner light, yellow-greenish. There was the stench of decay about it. Two burning red eyes she recalled so well from her dreams watched every flicker of her features, every move she made.

It was about ten feet tall, and had obviously once been very beautiful. Thick, curly golden hair covered its head, and the tall form was well-muscled. Two wings that must have once been huge and powerful grew from its back. Once it had been angelic—but not any longer.

It was as if the creature had been made of plastic and left too close to a terrible fire. The wings were twisted, useless for flying now. One shoulder was lower than the other, and warped forward, giving it a hunched appearance. Its skin, once clear and glowing with health, was now blotched, and in places blackened and rotting. But its face was the worst.

The once-handsome features had been wrenched out of their normal positions, as if some almighty hand had gripped its face and twisted it to the left. The mouth was crooked, the nose splayed, the left eye dragged across almost to the ear. Wrinkled skin, badly burned, overlay it all. The hair was stunted, burned, dead.

The right side of the demon's face was perfect, giving the left a worse horror.

"Now . . ." it said, in that hated voice. "Now, at last, I shall feed. . . ."

TWENTY

Sharon was too sickened by the sight of the creature to be as frightened as she had expected. It was so mutilated, so horrible, that she almost felt pity for it. Except that it was clearly just as mutilated inside.

With an odd clarity of thought, she remembered what Mr. Williams had told her. Demons enjoy destroying anything pure or beautiful. She realized that there was more to it than that: Demons try to warp the rest of the universe as badly as they are. They wanted to drag beauty, goodness, purity down to the same terrible level as themselves.

Sharon also realized something else: She knew the demon's name.

"Keriog!" she managed to cry out, with the last of her strength. "You're Keriog!" The name from the two paintings in Travis's scrapbook.

The two burning eyes focused sharply on her. "So," the voice whispered, "you are not so stupid, after all. You have named me."

Seizing on what Mr. Williams had told her, Sharon called out: "I have named you, Keriog. And, because I know your name, you must listen."

Keriog threw back his misshapen head and laughed. Because of the twisted features, this was not a pleasant sound. "Ah, another who believes that old tale," he mocked. "That knowing the name of a demon gives you power over it." He shook his head. "It doesn't." Sharon felt her waning hopes dashed, and then saw the demon's eyes fix onto Travis, who had inexplicably stopped. She saw that he looked scared.

"But," Keriog added thoughtfully, "it does give you one advantage. Knowing my name, you may make a deal with me."

"A deal?"

"Yes." The demon's good right hand reached down, plucking the knife from Travis's frozen fingers. "A deal. The same deal that this young man made with me." He laughed, cold fire in the sound. "If you offer me a sacrifice, I will give you whatever you desire."

"A sacrifice?" Sharon echoed, not understanding.

"Come, child," Keriog hissed. "Don't be so stupid. I will spare your delicious little life—and give you anything you name—if you give me a sacrifice." He pointed the knife directly at Travis. "*His* life."

Sharon was chilled to her core. "You want me to kill him?"

"Well?" the demon asked. "He will kill *you* if you don't. I'm giving you your only chance. Kill him, give me his blood, his life-force."

"No!" Travis cried, terror-stricken but unable to move. "No! Keriog, you promised me!"

The demon reared up, hissing. Sharon could see that he had long, pointed nails on each huge hand. "Spare me your whining!" it said angrily. "It amuses me to offer her the same choice you were given." Then the eyes returned to stare at Sharon. "Well?"

Despite her revulsion, Sharon could feel the power of the idea. Travis was going to kill her, but she could have her revenge on him. She could kill him and save herself. . . . Hatred for Travis began to cloud her mind, and she could almost feel the thrust of the knife into him. . . .

"No!" she cried, drawing back from the thoughts. "No, never!" Abruptly, the cloud of fury and hatred lifted from her mind. She began to understand what Keriog had been doing. Though Travis's soul would not have been as appealing to him, corrupting Sharon by getting her to kill would have more than made up for that slight loss. "You," she whispered to Keriog. "You tried to make me agree. It was you."

"No," he said softly. "No. I cannot cause within you what is not there to begin with. It was *your* evil that I called on. It was your hatred that almost drove you to me. You fight it down, but there is some of me inside of you, as there is in every human being."

"But I fight it," she said. She grasped the chain of the crucifix about her neck and pulled it from the top of her tattered leotard. It gleamed in the light from the demon, and she saw Keriog flinch in pain as she held it up. "I have a choice. And I chose good, not evil!"

"Then you chose death!" the demon snarled. It threw the knife downward, and Sharon screamed, expecting to feel it thud into her flesh. Instead, at the last second, Travis jerked up his hand and caught the weapon. His eyes gleamed in anticipation, and he licked his lips.

"Take her," Keriog breathed. "Take her—*now!*"

Freed from his paralysis, Travis jerked forward. Sharon, unable to rise and run, could only hold up her hands in helpless defense. Perhaps the cross . . .

"I'm not a devil," Travis told her with a snarl. He grabbed the cross, and with a yank tore it from around her neck. "It doesn't hold me at bay." With a laugh, he tossed it into the bushes.

Helpless, terrified, Sharon didn't even have the strength to scream as Travis lunged for her. She rolled slightly aside, and the knife narrowly missed transfixing her heart. She heard it rip through her costume and felt a sharp pain down her ribs. She cried out, trying to get to her feet.

Cursing, Travis pulled the knife free and came for her again. His knee knocked her to the ground, and she grunted in pain. She struggled with him, grabbed the wrist with the knife in it. His face contorted, he spat out curses. Dizzy from her running and the pain, she felt him break her weak grip, and saw, blurred, his hand rise to gather the strength for the fatal thrust to her heart. . . .

TWENTY-ONE

Then, suddenly, something slammed into him. Travis toppled over, and the weight was lifted from Sharon. Giddily, she struggled to get up. She barely had the strength to move, and then she felt arms around her, helping her.

"Girl, what *is* that thing?" Chiku whispered, shuddering, looking up at Keriog. She may have believed Sharon's story, but nothing could have prepared her to face what she was now seeing. Her shock and fear were written starkly across her face.

"Chiku! Thank goodness . . . That's him, the demon that wants me dead," Sharon managed to say. She struggled, and curled up in a sitting position. "Chiku, how . . . ?"

"Larry clued us in," her friend replied, not taking her eyes from the demon. "Travis beat him up, to make sure he'd keep me away from you. We tried calling to warn you, but there was no answer. So we rushed over. We found the study a wreck, the windows open, and the trail leading here."

Sharon's head had cleared enough for her to see what was happening. Chiku's father had jumped Travis, knocking him down, and they were fighting over the knife. Strength began to trickle back into her. But, even with Chiku and Mr. Williams here— there was still Keriog to be faced.

Curiously, the demon seemed unmoved by his disciple's fight. The twisted grin was still on his face —he was enjoying watching Travis getting thrashed. Sharon realized that the demon fed on pain and fear, no matter who it came from. It didn't care who won the fight, as long as someone was killed. . . .

Though Travis was younger and desperate, Mr. Williams was putting up a good fight. Obviously he hadn't been an academic all of his life, because he knew some pretty nasty moves. Sharon winced as the two men kept landing blow after blow on each other. She looked again at Keriog, and saw him basking in the emotions that the fight was producing. As if he were growing larger . . .

"We've got to stop the fight," she gasped. "It's just making Keriog stronger." She got to her feet and started to look around for anything to use as a weapon.

She felt terrible. She was cut and bruised, and her costume was in shreds. But she fixed her mind on one thing: stopping the fight. With a cry, she finally saw what she needed: a piece of broken branch, about four feet long. It took all of her energy to lift it, while Chiku watched, uncomprehending.

Sharon staggered over to where Travis and Mr. Williams were locked in combat, and waited for her chance. As soon as Travis presented a clear target, she swung the branch, smacking it down hard on his right arm.

With a hoarse yell, Travis dropped his knife, and Chiku's father pushed him clear. Travis fell backward, his arm hanging limply by his side. His handsome features were marred with blood from a cut over his eye, by the hatred on his face and the fear in his eyes. Panting, Mr. Williams stood up, hunched over him.

"You rotten punk," he gasped out. "Make one move, and I'll cripple you for life."

"Er . . . Dad," Chiku said, grabbing his arm. Shaking his head to clear the effects of the fight, he followed her gaze, and stiffened in shock.

Keriog, aware that he was once again the center of attention, laughed. "You humans are so entertaining," he breathed. "You really do keep me most amused, you know."

"Dear God!" Mr. Williams exclaimed.

"Sorry," Keriog mocked. "You're not even close." He loomed over them, drinking in their fear and revulsion. "Out of the frying pan and into the fires of hell . . ."

"No!" Chiku's father groped into his pocket and pulled out a crucifix. He might be a lecturer in mythology, but he had never in his wildest dreams imagined he'd ever be faced with a creature like this. . . . It took all of his self-control, clearly, to hold the cross steadily in front of him.

For the first time, Sharon saw both pain and fear on Keriog's grotesque face. He threw up an arm to shield his face, hissing and spitting. He hadn't been affected by Sharon's cross earlier, since Travis had been between them and had snatched it from her. Now, he took several paces backward, reaching forward with his other hand, snarling.

"So, human, you know something about me," the demon growled. It was managing to overcome the pain it felt, and the burning eyes glared out again. "But that cross can protect only yourself. Not your daughter . . ." With a warped grimace of delight, Keriog staggered toward Chiku.

Terrified, the black girl backpedaled quickly. She reached to her neck, drawing out another crucifix. Again Keriog snarled and backed away in fear and frustration. Then his glowing eyes centered on Sharon. Sharon realized that Travis had taken her cross and thrown it away.

Keriog's smile twisted in pleasure. "But you have nothing, nothing to protect you from me," he said softly. "And if that incompetent fool can't deliver you to me, then I shall break your bones and drink your blood myself. . . ." With a sudden lunge, his huge fist closed about her.

Sharon's scream was choked into silence. His touch burned like fire into her skin. The stench of death was stronger, and she felt the oversized hand begin to squeeze. . . .

"No!" Mr. Williams cried, stepping forward. "You cannot take her! You have no right! You have no claim on her!"

Keriog's grip relaxed slightly, and Sharon could manage a small breath, then another. She hurt all over and wanted desperately to simply faint, or die, and have it all finished with, once and for all. But she willed herself to stay conscious.

"I can do as I want," Keriog insisted.

Shaken and scared as he was, Chiku's father took another step toward the demon. "You have no claim on her. You can only take directly what is yours. Let her go."

"She *is* mine," Keriog howled. Drops of saliva dripped onto her, and they stung like acid. Sharon writhed in his grip. "She was promised to me, and has been delivered."

"No," Mr. Williams said forcefully. "Travis couldn't deliver her. She is still alive. She is not yours. Let her go."

Keriog wavered, staring down hungrily at Sharon. "She is mine," he insisted. "I have a deeper claim on her than *his* promise of delivery. Her father was mine, and she is his daughter—evil dwells within her. That makes her mine to claim."

His eyes tore into her, stripping her emotions bare. Sharon writhed in embarrassment, humiliation, and agony as her darkest fears were dragged out from her. She remembered the desire to kill that had almost overcome her. The wish for Travis's blood, his death at her hands . . . "No!" she screamed. "No! I didn't do it! I didn't! I won!"

Then that memory vanished, to be replaced by worse ones. The secret fantasies about Travis came back to taunt and haunt her. Keriog laughed, exposing her dreams to the onlookers. Sharon tried to close her eyes. The demon was right—she was evil in her heart. Bitterly, she knew that he had a territorial claim on her soul.

"No!" Chiku yelled. "No! It's not her fault! She didn't know!" She ran at the demon, shaking her fist in his face. "She's innocent, damn you!"

Abruptly, Sharon realized that the others could see somehow what she was going through. They weren't condemning her—they were there to support her. Astonished by Chiku's courage and fury directed at Keriog, Sharon found herself daring to hope. Perhaps it was possible to defeat him. . . .

The huge hand opened, and she fell to the ground. It was impossible for her to hurt any more than she already did. She groaned and felt Chiku grab her, protectively placing herself between her friend and the demon. Sharon cleared her vision and looked up at Keriog.

He seemed smaller, more twisted than before, though not by much. His features contorted by more than the usual disfigurement, he was backing away, shaking his head. She could see fury on his terrible face, and she realized that Chiku and her father were right: Keriog could not harm her directly. He had no power over her.

"It's over," Sharon said, knowing that it was true. "It's over, Keriog. I'm free of you at last!"

"Perhaps," the demon hissed. Its eyes, showing a mixture of pain and venom, fastened onto Travis. The young man had been nursing his injured arm, and keeping deliberately very quiet. "But I have been summoned, and someone has to pay my price."

Suddenly aware of what Keriog had in mind, Travis uttered a desperate yell and tried to crawl to safety. Keriog laughed and reached out.

"No!" Sharon screamed. "Leave him alone!"

Keriog hesitated and smiled, almost wistfully. "Pleading for the one who would have gutted you like an animal, girl? Ah, such fierce emotions! You would have been a feast indeed for me to enjoy in the long nights in the pit. Your goodness would have sustained me for eons. But . . ." He sighed, and looked back at Travis, who was almost fainting in terror. "Beggars can't be choosers. I take what and where I can—even a disgusting little morsel like this. . . ."

Travis screamed again, and then Keriog struck. The clawed hand pierced him through and lifted. The long talons stuck out bloodily from the youth's back, and Travis howled in agony and terror. Then Keriog closed his fist, crushing. There was an audible snap, and then the demon shuddered. The hand opened, and the shattered, blood-soaked body of Travis fell back to the ground.

With a final wicked laugh, Keriog vanished.

TWENTY-TWO

Mr. Williams, sporting several cuts, managed to walk slowly over to the two girls. Without a word he removed his coat and dropped it over Sharon's shoulders. She winced as the weight and texture of it rubbed against her cuts and bruises. Shivering, she drew the coat tightly about her body.

Chiku's father crossed to Travis's shattered body. He shook his head, half in sorrow, half in disgust. "Well, he paid the price," he said. "I just hope I can think of some good story to explain *those* wounds to the police."

Sharon nodded numbly. "Is it over?" she asked.

"Yes," he said. "Yes, it's over. Without Travis, Keriog has lost his last link to you. I think your dreams will be free of him from now on."

"Good." Sharon sighed. "Because I think I'm going to spend the rest of my life asleep. I'm exhausted."

"Poor thing," Chiku said in a motherly tone.

"Come on, let's get back to the car. We'll drive you home." Her eyes twinkled. "Unless you still want to go to the dance. You'd be a hit in that costume."

"Well, it's nice to see you haven't lost your sense of humor," Sharon remarked. "I think mine's completely dead. Among other things." She stared at Travis. "I can't help feeling sorry for him, even if he did want to kill me." She sighed. "He was my half brother, you know. Same father, but a different mother."

Mr. Williams joined them again. "Then he was his father's son. Wilde gambled with the devil and lost. So did Travis. But you're your mother's daughter—you wouldn't give in."

Sharon nodded, and they started to walk slowly back through the woods. Mr. Williams seemed to know where he was going, and Chiku helped Sharon. She had kept the branch she had found, using it as a crutch. Still, it was a long, painful trip, and Sharon began to realize just how much the events of the evening had taken out of her.

They were almost back to the house when it happened. Something large, scaly, and green emerged from the bushes on the side of the path. Sharon could just make out a mouth full of teeth, a tail, and spines that stuck out of the creature's back.

She had faced enough for one evening, and this horror emerging from the gloom simply annoyed her. Hardly thinking, she lashed out with the branch, and heard it hit the monster fairly hard in the midriff. It gave a squeal of pain and collapsed backward onto the ground.

"Hey," she heard Larry say from inside the thing. "What's with you?"

Sharon's heart stopped pounding, and she looked closely at the creature. It registered that this wasn't some supernatural entity—just Larry in a Godzilla costume.

"Sorry," she managed to say. "Just bad timing on your part."

With Chiku's help, Larry managed to regain his feet. Still bewildered, he complained: "Will somebody please tell me what is going on? You guys just lit out of the car and left me there. I've been looking for you ever since. Then Sharon whacks me with a stick. What is this, pick on Larry night?"

Chiku laughed. "Believe me, Larry—you wouldn't believe me." She snuggled up next to the scaly costume. "Just stay close, okay? I'd be happier."

Hardly able to believe his luck, Larry just grunted and shuffled closer to her.

Sharon looked at Mr. Williams, who just shrugged. "Why do I get the impression," he asked her, "that I may end up seeing a lot more of this little monster?"

"Trust me," she answered. "There are worse things. Lots of them." Then she smiled, her heart free of the terrors at last. "But they're just nightmares . . . which I won't be having anymore."